# LIVE FROM THE TRENCHES

# LIVE FROM THE TRENCHES

A Novel By

**MILLENNIUM REEDZ
&
TRAVIS RAMSEY**

PUBLISHER'S NOTE:

This book is a work of fiction. It is not meant to depict, portray, or represent any particular real person. All the characters, incidents, and dialogues are the products of the author's imagination and are not to be construed as real. Any references or similarities to actual events, entities, real people, living or dead, or to real locales are intended to give the novel a sense of reality. Any similarities in other names, characters, entities, places, and incidents, are entirely coincidental. All rights reserved, including the right of reproduction in whole or part in any form.

All Copyrights Reserved 2024 Millennium Reedz & Travis Ramsey

# Table of Contents

Acknowledgements ................................................. vii
Demon Time - Donald Reynolds ........................... 1
Intro - Millennium Reedz ..................................... 16
The Ultimate Confession - Tranquil Justice ...... 19
A Man's Touch - Travis Ramsey ......................... 35
Shark Food - Millennium Reedz ......................... 42
Baltimore Love Story - @Djay_amazin .............. 46
Pledge Allegiance 2 - Millennium Reedz .......... 54
Overnight Success - Reggie West ....................... 57
Dear Cancer - Tranquil Justice ............................ 64
Scammerz With Hammerz - Meezy .................... 71
The Realest Ever - Millennium Reedz ................ 85
Super Grimmie - Millennium Reedz .................. 90
Escaping Death 2 - Tranquil Justice .................... 93

Trap .................................................................. 107

Terror On Line 1 - Millennium Reedz ............. 112

10 Finger Discount - Millennium Reedz ......... 116

Living For Real in the 21st Century -
Millennium Reedz ............................................... 120

Safe Haven - Millennium Reedz ....................... 130

Blondie ................................................................ 135

# Acknowledgements

**DONALD REYNOLDS:**

First and foremost, much thanks to the Most High. Then, there's my team of love and support that has never failed me. And without the fans of course, this movement wouldn't be worth pushin'. Soldier salute to Urban Drip Magazine, the supreme voice of urban news and entertainment. Follow me @RealUrbanDrip

**MEEZY:**

To follow Money Meezy on all social media platforts :

Facebook - Redbottom Clerk

Instagram - @Mezzy100

*Scammerz With Hammers* (the book coming soon)

## REGGIE WEST:

I want to thank Allah for even making this thing possible for creating Ali. I want to thank all you niggas that step from the time Lonnie passed into keeping his name alive y'all know who you are. Aint got to put no names on that. Forever 1204 stepper. Free my brother Mr. Keep dat you will be home soon they cage you but not your mind. Thanks to my two girl cousins Keda & Coo-coo. Y'all made my fed bid easy can't wait to return my love. All in all my son Lonnie West I can't wait to get back home to you. No matter what no one says remember dad loves you. For my pops I just want to be at them gates when they let you out. My mother Brina Baker you don't got to cry and worry about me no more I'm out of the streets. FCI Beckley: Matt Mahone, Melvin Hill, JJ, Big Man, Bobby Tario, Patch head, COE, Amp Bo, Tanka, Chico Tony Tony, Dorrell, and a lot more man I know we don't see eye to eye but deep down I have unconditional love for y'all. For all my sister and brother y'all know where we stand all 9 of y'all. Mama was a rolling stone Lol. Real Urban Drip Magazine, GMG. Cory Reed thats my guy and I put my all into that guy for a whole month straight he stands on business Gorgeous Money Getters is a brand you can trust. He made me push hard day in and day out when I wanted to give up he ain't give up on me so thanks bro. From Tampa to Shark City. DJ_Amazin thanks for jumping in this at the last minute but you made it. From Tampa to B-more. Tavaris Ramsey my cellmate nigga you know we lock-in 4 life. Thanks for teaching and holding them talks with me. That's the Georgia hero, Trapp. And you know I got to shoutout the #1 seller man keep grinding hard work pays off. And to you haters heep hating I'ma do me. Shoutout to my wife Alicia West you hold me down and people thought you would fall off they fell off when I first came to jail you're still here. I might get on your last nerve. But I want the best for us until death call my name. Bangout, Upone, Lock, Dooley, Fatboy, Kj, Sam, ED Dash, Luther, Micheal, Free Von, Dontae, Lil Louise, both Nerdos, Tarus. Man yall all our family got man. Ali Mceachin from Fayetteville North Carolina my nigga knew him 3 months b4 he went home that a real nigga 4 life. Also no cap I can go on and on all day. but I'ma leave yall with this love to my whole campaign. This is not the last time you will see my name on a book. So be looking for author

Reggie West, that sounds crazy right but it's true. I live a wild life, it's time to tell that story love into my pen hit a piece of paper. RIP Lonnie B, J-Mack, P-Dub, Deon, bumpa, Cash, and Britt, love y'all.

## DJ_AMAZIN:

I wanna thank Allah for giving me the power to write this wonderful short story. Second my kids, family, and friend be on the lookout for my next one "Rich Sex." Follow me on Instagram @DJay_Amazin

## MILLENNIUM REEDZ:

I would like to first and foremest thank God, for him giving me the power and strength to open my eyes each morning. He has blessed me with a miraculous gift and I am just along for the journey. Next I would like to give absolute salutes to all thses authors in this book. The Urban Drip Doc, Reggie, Tranquil Justice, DJ Amazin, Meezy. I also appreciate all the support, wisdowm and authenticity all throughout this project. Last but not least I would like to give thanks to my exceptional GMG apparel and marketing team, with all respects. This brand has helped catapuly my vision beyond my imagination. Please follow me on my self-publishing journey and subscribe to my blog, and social media accounts.

**Instagram:** @Gorgeous_Money_Getter

**Facebook:** GorgeousMoneyGetter

**Email:** Millennium971@Yahoo.com

**TAVARIS RAMSEY:**

First of all I wanna thank God, as I do daily. (Reguardless), because my current situation will not be my permanent desination. Now thank my mom dukes, my world Hattie Ramsey, thank you for giving birth to something that God loves (d. Truth), cause (I am dat) you and Joe did that. 8-21-77 A lion was born. Meet the Leo. Now shout out to my brother Twon G (Stand for too, win, or nothing, gunning) He calls us the boys in the hood. I'ma Baltimore bandit, Washington Wilkes. Dubb Dubb 4 life. Crazy on purpose nigga. Big ups to that guy Doc. Donald Reynolds who makes this possible. The plug for readers etc. Loving that Urban Drip magazine. That boi Reggie West, Tampa's lil boxing star. Mr. Fuck it swing first think 2nd. I love you my guy. That guy Corey Reed, CEO of GMG Gorgeous Money

Getters, the brand is out their people tune in for "Live in the kitchen 2" My two sons MTO Trapp lok him up on IG, songs on soundcloud, Iheartradio Etc. Lil Jay I'm proud of them daddy loves y'all. Last but never least Texas Bee Ramsey, an angel from heaven that got my back 4 life. I'll never get scoliosis. I love you the ones I didn't mention, I love y'all too just out of space. Peace.

**Facebook:** TrappMrGoRamsey

**TRANQUIL JUSTICE:**

For many years I've let my family and community down, in their world. I was like this little demon with no horns, that's how much of a nightmare I was in their everyday life. Involving myself in organized crimes, charges piling up like leaves and throwing bail money away like ballers in V.I.P clubs. I never left the streets any breaks. Now being incarcerated in Federal custody, I use my pen and paper as a sunlight of relief to overshine this darkness inside of me, and let this ink coming out of this pen be the voice of my pain. The same way I cause many griefs and sadness in my community and family's heart and faces. Now I am using this ink as a gift of wisdom to overshine their griefs and sadness, with joy, greatness, and happiness. By repaying them with great published stories and screenplays. To my grandma Fortune Jean-Pierre, uncle Daniel Jean-Pierre, Snoogika Fanfan, Prince Fanfan, James, my mom Renette. My aunt Adeline, Liline, Edmonde, David, Pouchon, Shayna and to the black community. Sorry for the madness and storms I put ya through. And to my loving sister Sandra Jean-Pierre may your soul rest in peace I love you. To these authors that walked in the same dark path that I was in and now find the light of wisdom to repay their families and communities with great stories of sunshine that will light up their journeys with joy and happiness. Reggie West, Millennium Reedz, Donald Reynolds, DJ Amazin, Mezzy, I salute you guys, you guys are great writers. Our fans and readers will forever remember these exciting stories in this epic novel here, because this is one of the greatest moves of all time where so many great authors come together to explore their readers journeys with joy and excitement, because this is an all in one epic novel that they will remember forever.

Millennium Reedz & Travis Ramsey

To our readers, thanks for the supports and thanks for believing in our writing skills and positivity. May the man above bless y'all.

# Demon Time
## Donald Reynolds

In the slimy, crime-ridden streets of Louisville, Kentucky, Cliford Johnson was mostly known as C-Money. With the volume of the stereo down low he pulled the stolen

Cadillac Escalade he was driving to a smooth stop at a traffic light. Next he flicked his half-smoked cigarette out of the cracked window. After scanning his rearview mirror for anything suspicious C-Money allowed his dangerous mind to drift away from the mission he was on tonight.

C-Money had been waist-deep in a criminal lifestyle of money laundering, drug and weapons trafficking and numerous acts of violence, not excluding murder. He closed his eyes and clutched the firm erection that had formed beneath the pistol that rested on his lap. When suddenly the angrily tooting of a Honda's horn brought him back to reality. He mashed the accelerator pedal down and soon steered into an upscale subdivision. Using the darkness of night to his advantage, C-Money was able to conceal his nefarious intentions.

After parking the SUV in the driveway of an empty home with a yellow rectangular-shaped 'For Sale' sign in the front lawn, C-Money slithered out and ambled across the street into the yard of a brick tri-level home, where he found cover while on his knees behind a manicured floriferous cluster of hedges and bushes. He glanced down at his watch, well-knowing that his mark would soon be arriving. The Latin rap music coming from inside the home piqued his attention. Crouched still, C-Money peered up into a slightly opened window, and noticed a long haired, young sexy Puerto Rican female with perky breasts dirty-dancing near-naked in front of a floor-to-ceiling mirror. She seemed to be admiring herself by the way the movements of her body. He observed the freak show which was arousing, but it wasn't a strong enough distraction to pry his mind off of what he came here to do tonight. So he waited.....

The headlights in the distance slowly grew closer. And soon enough, the sleek pearl-white Mercedes parked not too far away in the driveway. Before the suit-wearing man could even fully exit his luxury vehicle C-Money was right there, his silencer-equipped pistol trained dead in the center of the man's forehead. "Didn't think this day would ever come, did you?" C-Money smiled, his teeth barely visible beneath the ski mask he was now donning.

"What... Who?"

"I'm not on the witness stand, no need tryin' to cross- examine me. Your days of practicing law is over. Enjoy your trip to hell motherfucka. I'll see you again, whenever I make it there."

"What? Wait! Listen, I got three-hundred grand cash in there. In my safe. Please! Take it, just let me live." A puddle

of urine formed at the feet of the prosecutor. "Please!" He trembled. "Who who sent you?"

Without mercy, C-Money twice, pulled the trigger. Two muted slugs tore through the federal prosecutor's face, crumpling him beside his

Mercedes Benz. Next, C-Money tummy-tucked the warm pistol and escaped in the exact same silent manner in which he came. During the ride home he decided that he would stop off at Tamika's house. It was closer in distance than his own home that he shared with Leslie, his lover and fiancé. Stashing the murder weapon there made perfect sense, plus Tamika's sex game was what he had been thinking about all day anyway, aside from his murder- for-hire contract that had now been fulfilled. He brought the SUV well below the speed limit and turned left down a shallow, dark path of Kentucky bluegrass.

***

The sharp sudden pain caused Leslie to bite her bottom lip and grip the bottom of her stomach. For a little while in bed, she tossed and turned, hoping that Cliford would come home soon. She didn't understand the ghetto life he lived, and much of it was shrouded in secrecy anyway; and maybe in that mystery it was what attracted her to Cliford. Leslie stood at her bedroom window now, she could feel the child in her womb doing back flips. The night seemed gloomy, low-hanging dark clouds were scudding across the sky, and the only thing that made the moment any brighter was the thought of their upcoming wedding. Leslie continued to caress her stomach, losing herself in matrimonial thoughts, not paying much attention to the breaking news story airing on the television nearby. Her unborn child was hyperactive tonight, before sitting on the edge of the bed she told the baby "Daddy'll be home soon, to feed you," Leslie giggled, because sex seemed to always calm the baby down. She crawled beneath the comforter, in need of sex and security.

***

Tamika answered the door like she always did, with a big wide smile, arms open wide, and ready to embrace C-Money. "Damn, you smell like gasoline," said Tamika releasing her embrace. Her dark-brown skin-tone sparkled beneath the dim candle lighting; her home smelled like French vanilla. Her eyes searched the soul of C-Money's eyes for clues, and her nipples hardened on contact as both his hands gripped her voluptuous ass.

"Yeah, well I had to start a small fire earlier," said C- Money. He walked past Tamika into her living room, plopping down on her leather sofa.

"Whatever." She moved her school books off of the other end of the sofa and sat on his lap. "You OK?" She continued to touch him.

"I'm cool, just dealing with my street shit." He eased up his pistol and set it on the coffee table. "You know how I get down."

"You been on your ninja shit, huh? Well I been studying for my bar the past couple days." She paused exhaling frustration.

Their eyes met, and revealed exactly at that moment how much they needed each other. It was one of them things that they both understood without the need for any clumsy words. C-Money's hands pulled Tamika closer, lifting up the Louisville Cardinal tank top she wore, exposing her full breasts, and large areolas that contrasted perfectly in tan and brown colors. "Mmm," moaned Tamika, feeling her breasts being sucked, and fondled; without hesitation, she reciprocated the pleasure, stroking his crotch, feeling his manhood growing.

"You right on time," she whispered into his ear, running her fingers through the roots of his dreads. "You fuckin' me right?" she cooed, tugging at his jeans, finally liberating his thick and lengthy member.

"Baby, you know–"

"Shh," moaned Tamika, pulling her boy shorts over at the crotch area and guiding C-Money's dick inside her moist tight hole. "Damn, why you make me wait so long for this good ding-a-ling?" Tamika's question was rhetorical, and an answer she didn't care about. She knew he was involved with another woman and was due to get married. Her wide hips continued to gyrate, faster, while her fingers clawed away, pulling up C-Money's shirt. Next, she began to bounce up and down. "Mm," she cooed, "Mmmmm-hmm," she shut her eyelids tight and allowed this night to consumer her. Mind, body and soul. She could feel C-Money's large hands squeezing her ass cheeks harder, making her take every inch he had to offer. "I'm about to orgasm," whispered Tamika. "Mmmm." It felt awesome being in control of C-Money's lustful desires. She continued to ride.

"Cum all over my dick," ordered C-Money. "This dick feel good?"

"Oh, shiiiit, baby, woooo!" With both hands, Tamika clenched C-Money's face and drove her tongue into his mouth. She could feel his penis throbbing deep inside her as they came together. That's when he gripped her shoulders and delivered a series of far-reaching thrusts.

BOOM! BOOM! BOOM!

Neither of them paid much thought to the pounding on the front door until a bursting of a spot light and laser beams shone through the windows of the French doors, where an army of para-military suit-wearing law enforcement officials stood aiming weapons.

"Fuck!" C-Money spun over, tossing Tamika onto the floor, clutching his pistol, "stay down!" He took careful aim. "Be still."

"What's going on?"

"Shut up!" he growled. "It's–" "Poleece! We have a –"

Before the officer of the law could announce his intentions or reasons for being here tonight, C-Money sent a dozen glass-shattering rounds his way. Three of those bullets hit home, and the return of gunfire sent Tamika's young naked body sprawling into an end table that flipped over.

The thundering of a helicopter in the sky hovering sounded off; through a thick cloud of dust and gun smoke, C- Money cracked open his eyes, finding Tamika. "Fuck. Babygirl? I'm so sorry they did you like this." He belly- crawled to her side and held her warm body in his arms. Blood poured out from a gaping bullet hole in her head. C- Money knew his fate would be the same or worse than hers. He was too cold of a criminal to cower or cry, even if he wanted to. Somehow he left a trace of his whereabouts. In the background dogs let off vicious barks. He placed the tip of his pistol up to his head and shut his eyes, hoping this was a bad dream. Just then Leslie's beautiful reflection appeared in the darkness of his imagination, as did the innocent unborn child he now visualized. His finger tightened around the trigger, at the same time he said a silent prayer, asking his maker to forgive him of his life of sin, and criminality.

\*\*\*

Leslie twisted from side to side, violently her arms swang back and forth. The bedroom felt like an inferno. "Ahhhh," she cooed, trembling....."Ahhh!" Her blonde-colored hair appeared pasted to her face, as perspiration dripped from her firm body. "Ahh, fuck me!" She chanted, finally snapping out of her sleep. She clutched her chest; her heart felt like it was about to jump through her ribcage. After catching her breath Leslie crawled out of bed, noticing the morning sunrays welcoming in a brand-new day. But Cliford had not returned home. She could have sworn she felt him thrusting deep inside her. Leslie could feel the wetness between her ass knowing now she'd had a wet dream. For a while she sat there, regaining her composure, and then headed for the shower. But she paused suddenly in her tracks. "What the hell!" There was blood. A whole lot of blood, it was racing down her thighs. "My God, noo!" Without hesitation, she darted into the bathroom, but the glimpse she caught of Cliford, and her cousin, Tamika's reflection on the morning news called her back before the TV set for answers. She held a hand on her broken heart.

Tears poured from Leslie's face as the newscaster detailed the horrific events of last night. She dropped to her knees, "God, why?" The blood continued to come down, but Leslie didn't care. "Why God?" She knew she had been nothing, but faithful, loving, supportive and caring. "Answer me, God, damnit!" She shut her eyes as if it would stop the torrential out-pouring of tears, and blood. And out of nowhere a familiar deep voice came into her divine realm of recognition.

"Sweetheart, please stop crying."

Leslie snapped open her eyelids, only to find the thin white-colored curtain covering the bedroom window flapping. "I'm so sorry Leslie that things happened the way they did. All them nights you prayed for me while I ran the streets got me going to a better place baby. I love you. And I'll always be with you. I need you to be strong, and live your life. I got our daughter, I'm taking her to be in heaven with me. If I can't be on earth to protect her, it's best she not be born. My time's up baby, our souls are being called home now. I love you."

"No! No!" shouted Leslie, "no!" She crawled toward the nightstand retrieving her cellphone, punching in 9-1-1.

"State your emergency?" answered the 9-1-1 operator.

"I need a paramedic at 123 Angel Lane, I'm having a miscarriage..."

**One Month Later....**

"Leslie, I need you to explain to me what is going on with you. I'm here to help you," said Doctor Rudolph, a curly-haired, mixed-heritage, psychotherapist with green eyes. It was like pulling teeth for her trying to get Leslie to open up about the recent tragedies she had experienced. "You can't heal what you don't reveal."

Leslie sat there, rocking back and forth, shoulders slumped forward, sniffling. The past month had been a horrific never- ending nightmare. Not to mention, today was the day she and Cliford would have been married, and headed off to the Bahamas for their honeymoon. She let off a slight groan and cuffed her tummy that had been growling like a monster all morning. Next, she fiddled with her engagement ring.

"Please, Leslie. Tell me –"

"Ok, give me a second," said Leslie. "For the past few weeks I haven't been able to sleep in spite of the medication I'm taking." She wiped a tear off her chin. "Every morning I wake up sore from head to toe, and especially everywhere in between. Meaning my vagina." She paused.

Doctor Rudolph handed her a sheet of scented tissue paper from a small package on her desk. Leslie accepted it and dabbed at her eyes. "Take as much time as you need."

"As I drift off to sleep at night, my fiancé appears, and he rips my thighs apart and violently makes love to me all night. He strangles me, and lets it be known that if I get involved with any other man he'll make my life a living hell."

The office filled with silence, and Doctor Rudolph sat up straight and looked Leslie square in the eye. "Incubus," she whispered, "Incubus is an evil spirit that enjoys having sex with women while they sleep." She paused. "Was your fiancé evil-spirited?"

"He was a demon." Leslie began to cry again. "But I prayed, and prayed for him." She clutched her stomach. "I swear I did."

"Not all prayers are answered, and wherever his resting place may be, he seems hell-bent on taking you with him for eternity."

"Doctor, I took a pregnancy test this morning....Twice. It came back positive, and since my miscarriage I haven't been with anyone." Leslie's brown eyes searched the face of Doctor Rudolph for more answers; a solution; an urban remedy or advice, yet at that moment, no response was received. After a couple of minutes of silence, Doctor Rudolph took a sip of her coffee that had gotten cold. She set the mug down. "Leslie, fear-driven thinking errors are telling your brain a story," she said. "And only you can change the narrative."

**7 MONTHS LATER.....**

With her trembling hands at ten-and-two o'clock on the steering wheel Leslie drove slow and cautiously. In her mind, that bordered the edge of insanity she continued to grapple with the fear of the unknown. In spite of her anxieties and fears she tried to process her reality; a dark reality that felt like death was calling her. Goosebumps rippled across her forearms as she drove on through the red light at a busy four-way intersection near downtown, Louisville. She never heard the explosion of the red dump truck that collided with her vehicle. The only thing Leslie saw was her life flashing before her eyes, as the scent of burning gasoline, and flames devoured all of her five senses, and soul. What remained alive in this realm of life was Cliford's seed, and Leslie's prayers. In no time, a demon was born.

**THE END.**

# Intro

## Millennium Reedz

***Excerpt from Live From The Kitchen**

It was a warm summer, late night, a little past 1 am. As the dark profound sky dazzled with stars, a Norfolk Southern freight train soared through the hood doing a buck twenty, nonstop. All you can hear was the loud screams as it passes. As the train shuffles away on it's tracks, you could hear voices, grunting and laughter. A few yards away men, teenagers and old heads hunched together, as if in a football huddle.

"Bite 'em girls."

"Big six!"

"Head pop!"

"Strike dice!"

The sounds of shaking dice filled the air. We were shooting C-Lo. As I'm arrogantly talking to the dice, as I shoot to a big four. I got a band down (a thousand dollars), so I got to beat the point.

Since elementary school I've been breaking dice games in the bathroom on lunch period. Vigorously shaking the dice, I blew into my fist and eventually roll 'em. The dice came out of my hand as if in slow motion. The bystanders were looking on in astonishment as triple ones turned up. It looked so gorgeous. The crowd went crazy like when Steph Curry hit a half court shot right before half-time.

"Double me up my boi, 2 bands," I said to the bank. Two dudes who ran the bank on this particular night.

Welcome to Shark City, VA, (also known as Norfolk). Where the water's deep and you gotta swim at your own risk! Ironically, it is a beautiful city, top three in the U.S. for having one of the most preeminent beaches, according to go-vacations.com. The beaches are majestic with jet skis and exotic women coming to visit twelve months out of the year. There is also a diverse community, with two gigantic malls, a late night life, and condos along thirty story buildings. The

Tidewater area is surrounded by two bodies of water, the Chesapeake Bay, connects directly to the Atlantic Ocean. Furthermore, it's right in the middle of the Seven Cities, a commute to six other cities within fifteen minutes.

# The Ultimate Confession

## Tranquil Justice

At home Terry was this little charming boy that his family was proud of and loved. Because nowadays it's hard to find too many black kids living in the ghetto with an educated head like Terry had on his shoulders.

Terry was pursuing to be a film director at Brooklyn College and Terry's best days at school were always Fridays, because it was his relief day where he didn't have to bother with other students clowning and picking on him for wearing the same clothes all week to school. His parents were trapped in a low budget income, they couldn't afford any new outfits for him, so Terry hated Monday through Thursday.

On Friday nights, Terry's grandmother would pick him up for church for Saturday morning because she was a Seventh Day Adventist. So Terry would spend the weekends with her and return back home to his parents on Sunday afternoon.

But between those two nights only, Terry was like a persistent roller coaster of agony to his grandma, because she'd always jump from her sleep to go rescue Terry from his nightmares and this Friday night was no different.

When she heard the loud horrifying scream, it startled her from her sleep. "Terry!" she sighed. She checked the alarm clock on the nightstand next to her head it was already 3:30 am. "Oh God," she whined when she figured she only had one hour and thirty minutes to be up and get ready for church, because she was the head ushering member at her deceased husband's church. So she had to be at the church at 7:30 am at the latest. Every Saturday morning her and Terry would wake up at 5 am, take showers, eat breakfast, get dressed, and the remaining time they'd spend driving and find parking.

"Ah! Ah! Leave me alone you monster! Get away from me you monster, I killed you already! You are dead...." Terry was next door in his sleep having the fight of his life in his nightmare with his demons.

That's another thing terry loved being at his grandma he'd have a whole room to himself to sleep in comfortably, her son Terrence had bought them a half a million-dollar, two storied brownstone house in Canarsie, the good part of Brooklyn. Abigail, Terry's mother, was Terrence's sister. Abigail and her mother fell apart because of the men she chose to frequent in life. Terry's father James has an alcohol problem when he get's drunk he'd brutally beat her and the consequence of it would always result with him spending some critically lengthy nights in jail, and Abigail's mom had always been thanking the Lord for Terry's gentle charm. She thinks that Terry was brought up different from his cruel dad. Because of the many nights she spent on her knees begging the Lord for a miracle.

"Terry! Terry!" she shouted while standing over Terry with her hand grasping his shoulder waking him up. "Terry!"

"Uh," Terry jumped out of his nightmare, his body was drenched in sweat and he was breathing hard. The lights in his room was on and it reflected the glistening sparks on the sweat running over his small light complexioned chest.

"Granny..?"

"Are you okay?" she asked.

"I think a witch was riding me in my sleep."

"Boy! You're only 19 years old what do you know about black magic?"

"That's what my mom and dad would say."

"Abigail and James barely know a thing or two about their own culture they've come from much less black magic, it's a miracle that you graduated high school before these two, so they couldn't have taught you enough."

"Anyway who is this person in your dreams you claimed that you killed Terry? Have you killed anybody? Because now you have been straining from his same nightmare for awhile now."

"Granny.....No!" Terry cried in horror, "it was only a nightmare! I've never even seen a gun before, much less used one."

"Anyway I think you should see a psych," she suggested, "later on at church I will introduce you to this lovely girl, you can talk to her about anything, she's a close friend of the family."

"Have I met her?" Terry asked.

"Yes, it's Fabienne."

"Oh. Uncle Terrance's girlfriend."

"You mean fiance, they should be getting married next summer," she corrected.

Fabienne was this stern, beautiful, dark complexion lady with a PhD in psychology. Fabienne has a twin sister named Fabiola and Fabiola was a lieutenant at the 69 Precinct from Canarsie who doesn't frequent church at all, but Fabienne didn't take it personal, she loves her sister for who she is.

Because Fabiola was having a hard time finding a good man, Fabienne would always tease her about so many successful great men she'd come across at her psych office. Out of the blue Terrence invited Fabienne on a trip over to Antigua where he's surprise her with a diamond ring. Of course since Fabienne was her own boss she didn't turn down Terrence's offer, Fabienne simply tossed the key to her office to her twin

Fabiola without her realizing the risk of her action and Fabiola was shocked at the request.

During Fabienne's absence, Fabiola herself asked for a week off from the precinct, and to her surprise she was successful at doing a great job mentoring her sister's patients, that's how Fabiola came across her first boyfriend, but things didn't quite work out well. Until she reminded herself her sister was running a psych office for crazy people. But however Fabiola found herself becoming fascinated with her sister's career, even when Fabienne had returned back from Antigua on Fabiola's days off at the precinct, she'd be the one seating on her sister's chair mentoring her patients, and the patients also admired her because Fabiola was extra gorgeous.

"You want the lights off?"

"No you can leave it on granny," Terry said when his grandma walked off, Terry flopped his head hard on the pillow in distress, only if she knew that her son Terrence was the one who'd created the monster in him.

Terrence was a Navy officer, after his two year contract he didn't renew for a third one, because him and his Russian buddy Povich had other plans. Povich's reason for joining the Navy was different from many people's. He needed to build a trust with the U.S. government in order to protect his father's mob organization from harm, and from there Povich and Terrence bonded and some how Terrence agreed to be a hitman for the mob. When Terrence returned back home he saw Terry as an opportunity since Terrence was well aware of his financial issues, so Terrence started to shower him with expensive clothes and money. He taught Terry how to fight in order to defend himself from the bullies at school. He taught Terry how to shoot a gun, little did Terry know he was already wrapped under his uncle's charm and found himself becoming an executioner and hit-man for him. And Terrence's promise to Terry was if he'd continue going to school and church with his mom and pretend to be the innocent good boy that everyone was familiar with, he would be safe, and would be looked out for him financially.

While Povich was the one cutting the checks, Terrence was the terrifying director behind Terry's screen in real life, and the dead people in Terry's nightmares were the worse characters that refused to spare granny a good nights sleep on the weekend.

That Saturday, later on after church, Terry's grandma went on to explain to Fabienne about Terry's nightmares, and Fabienne was generous enough to offer her services, she handed her a business card along with a scheduled appointment of twice a week therapy for Terry to follow through with.

When Terry returned back home on Sunday afternoon, his advised his mother about his psychology therapy appointment sessions with Fabienne, and Abigail was furious when her mom didn't ask her for her permission. Abigail thought this was a low blow coming from her mom for thinking she could raise her own son better than she can, because she lived in poverty. But Terry figured it was a mother and daughter clash so he pursued on with Fabienne and his grandmother's request without his mom Abigail's blessings.

The next day after school Terry rushed to downtown Brooklyn at Fabienne's office. When he got there Terry noticed a whole different outlook about Fabienne. She had a nose ring, her manicured hands and pedicured feet were perfectly polished in red, she even wears a small gold chain to her ankle and her clothes were extra tight to her skin. Her hair was perfectly spread to her shoulders. Her whole sudden naughty appearance startled Terry because he knew the Bible forbid children to behave in such a sinful manner. But Terry hasn't yet met the other half of Fabienne, her twin sister.

"Fabienne," Terry sounded shocked.

"You may have a seat," Fabiola ordered him. The bright office was upscale and polished with a beautiful bronze colored marble table, a glass bookshelf, a portable AC, and electric water falling and mahogany seats. Terry pulled one of the mahogany chairs and sat, his elbows on the marble table in front of him.

Fabiola walked around the table to Terry and sat some paperwork in front of him to sign, the sweet aroma of her guilty perfume from Versace baptized Terry's nostrils into a pool of paradise.

"Please sign everywhere you see an X."

"So Terry," Fabiola began saying, "I read through your file and you've confirmed that a witch has been riding you in your sleep. I am kind of curious please be more specific about what's been causing these nightmares?" Fabiola asked, she was not interested on having a seat herself her long shapely legs and voluptuous hips were happily sashaying across the room, which made Terry a little intimidated by her beauty.

"My body will be tense from my sleep while I'd feel a set of hands suffocate my body into bed, my eyes would be open, while I shout and scream, fighting. But my body would remain suffocating from the sets of hands," Terry replied while jotting down his names through the papers.

"And how often does this happen?"

"Every time I sleep."

"Even when taking a nap during daytime?" Fabiola asked.

"Yes."

"What do you see in your sleep?"

"Dead people."

"And you are..." Fabiola dragged the words under her tongue while reaching for Terry's folder and scanned through it for some sort of something specific. "19 right?" she asked finally finding her voice again.

"Yes," Terry replied. Fabiola got quiet for a second. She unbuttoned the top two buttons from the shirt she wore to reveal the apple shape from her perfect 32 DD cups hiding behind the black Victoria's Secret bra she wore. I guess this was the seductive tactics she's been using to seduce her sister's clients. This was not her profession anyway who were they to judge?

"Um, Terry have you killed anybody before?" she asked. Terry's gaze was caught in between Fabiola's shapely DD cups and her question. "Terry do you mind answering the question? Please?"

"Um," Terry was startled back to reality. "I think--- I think- I should go," he jumped from his seat and rushed out of the office.

"Is everything okay? Make sure you're here on Wednesday," she yelled after him. When Fabiola turned towards the glass bookshelf, the reflection of her badge was staring back at her. "Damn," she hissed. "Did he catch that?" she asked holding a firm grip on the police badge.

On Wednesday when Terry returned back to Fabienne's psych office for his next session Fabiola was looking more attractive than ever and this time she has tricks up her sleeves for

Terry. This is it that Terry was the only patient of her sisters that she was interested in? Fabiola feels it's more to this than just therapy.

"The last time you were here why did you run out? Did something scare you?" Fabiola asked. "Did you see something you weren't supposed to?"

"No," Terry calmly responded.

"Are you sure?"

"Positive."

"Please forgive my naughty behavior the last time I saw you. Are you a virgin?" Terry put his head down in shame. "It's okay Terry, you're doing great, you don't need any of that headache right now. No baby mama drama."

"So," she sighed, "how about we pick up right where we left off last time we met. Have you killed anybody before?"

"Look," she said tossing her hands as a sign of being reluctant. "If you don't feel comfortable or trust me enough to talk about it, it's okay, but on the real I'm the only person that can help those demons get away from your sleep. There is a reason why your grandmother assigned you here with me to get you help," Fabiola was willing to try anything she could to get this one answer from out of Terry's mouth.

"Yes," he confessed out of the blue, and Fabiola was shocked how fast the unexpected answer came out of his mouth. She was frozen on her seat, there she was a lieutenant from a precinct sitting across from a killer and she didn't know what to say next.

"It's okay, we all make mistakes, none of us are perfect. We live in a world full of sins," Fabiola assured him, "this is what I want you to do. I want you to go home and reminisce about the murder or murders you have committed. I want you to confess about everything to me on your next appointment without missing a bit. Is that fair?" she asked with a friendly smile across her angelic face.

"Cool," Terry agreed.

"Now go home and get you some rest," Fabiola cheered, when knowing that her impulse was at last going to result in an arrest. But she'd rather play it this way only to gain Terry's trust.

Friday came by, Terry's grandmother came to pick him up for church on Saturday. Terry had a peaceful night with his grandma. When the morning hit Terry was anxious and couldn't wait to see Fabienne at church. His mysterious future wife, also his uncle's fiance, because Terry was head over heels for Fabienne.

When Terry saw her at church Fabienne's innocent sisterhood church appearance threw him off, because it was not the same as the attractive naughty sex appeal she had at the psych office. But still that didn't push Terry away. When Terry saw Fabienne he went for a hug but this time inappropriately grabbed her buttocks, Fabienne was shocked and didn't know how to embrace the embarrassing situation so she simply brushed it off. Even Terrence noticed the foul play from Terry he simply shook his head in a disgusted manner.

When Monday hit Terry rushed to Fabienne's psych office for his therapy session. There was Fabiola with hells on and a skin tight sun dress patiently waiting on Terry's arrival. Fabiola talked Terry into confessing about every murder he'd committed, she recorded everything from A to Z, but one thing terry did well through his whole murder confession he never mentioned his uncle Terrence's name. As far as Povich, Terry didn't know who he was and never once met or heard of him. After the ultimate confession from Terry, Fabiola invited him out the next day, for lunch.

When the next day hit the street was quiet, the 12 o'clock afternoon sky seemed sour and dark, but the rain wasn't pouring hard enough to avoid Terry from meeting up with Fabienne. When Terry got to 83rd and Flatlands, the Dunkin Donuts parking lot was empty and not one other car was in the parking lot. Terry proceeded on towards the donut shop, he scanned through the double glass door inside of the shop for Fabiola among the regular clothed civilians that were in there enjoying their meal. She was no where in sight, and the instant Terry reached for the door and stepped foot inside of the donut shop. A ton of weapons were drawn towards him coming from all directions.

FREEZE They all yelled in unison. Now there goes the police siren whirling from everywhere with cop cars flooding the lot. Where were they all hiding? Terry wished he could answer that.

Fabiola's exotic shape stepped out of an unmarked black Impala undercover cop car wearing blue pants with a white long sleeve button down shirt and yellow stripes ran across both shoulders.

"Terry you're under arrest for multiple counts of homicide. You have the right to remain silent and anything you say can be used against you in the court of law," Fabiola rumbled under her breath, the same necklace Terry thought he saw around her neck on his first therapy session was dangling around her neck still with her badge hanging to her breast.

"Surprise!" she cheered, while swinging the chain around her neck, showing off the badge.

"Shit," Terry cursed, while getting to his knees with his hands and fingers locked behind his head.

He should have known......Police love donuts.

# A Man's Touch

## Travis Ramsey

My first stripper's name was Shauntae A.K.A Boitae but now they call her Puchii. She had the smoothest golden brown skin that I'd ever seen. Her measurements were 40-28-36, Double D cups, and she knows how to throw it. She even got a tat that says "Trapp's bitch" on her ass. When she'd strut even the other hoes had to admire from her lucious smile to her ideal frame and even her toes were pigioned. She lives in Atlanta now, and she only dates bigtime rappers and the prestigious.

We use to bump heads 13 deep in the Esurgen, on our way to make that money. It's funny but I remember when I first had one hoe, then I grew my stable to thirteen of the most gorgeous hoes in the DubDub (Washington Wilkes, GA). Cream was my head honcho, she runs her hoes and I ran mine. I was supposed to fuck with her too, but we just kept it all business with complete professional adequacy. Cream would put the plan down to the hoes and made sure the girls were charging the customers the full price and making sure they use condoms and stayed money driven. With Cream's 8 hoes, and with my 13, together we built a stable that was running neck to neck with Hugh Heffner. I kept shit loud like a pickle jar smell. There was one time we had two fascinating hoes, their names were 6'9 and Sunshine. 6'9 was just like her name and she had an ass that people thought she hid soccer balls in her pants. Shorty's ass was that fat. However, more so, Sunshine was a short, thick, voluptuous hoe, that would let niggas pound her goodies for perpetual hours and she always wanted more. All the girls would say that she has a while liver which sent her hormones into overdrive. On one particular night 6'9 and Sunshine did a breathtaking trick with a 15" purple dildo that had the entire audience in complete feverish captivation. At once upon a time Boitae and I started out in houses, then soon after that we stepped up our game, and rented out a sports bar and I named it "A Man's Touch." Trapp's Kitchen was ringing bells and everybody knew it. My motto was ballers come and play, stragglers stay away and niggas respected my establishment, and what I had going on. Now when I tell you Trapps's Kitchen was the shit, ok, now once inside there was a 40 x 60" landscape all together making the sports bar have a happy go-friendly atmosphere. There were 6 flat screen 60" Tv's hanging from the walls. We played sporting events non-stop. Also we had 6 pool tables for the so-called shooters and pool sharks. Even more so, there were 12 Vap slot machines throughout the bar. Seemingly if a nigga wanted a suck or a fuck, my hoes would fix you up. You pay the ticket, and then you pick the hoe, you want and take her down to my hoe house. And also if you something hot to eat, that's where Trapp's Kitchen comes into play. Trapp's Kitchen has the best chicken wings in the country. We also sold hot dogs, beef patties, BBQ turkey burgers, sizzling French fries, plant based burgers for the veggie eaters, plus a wide selection of fresh fish. The drinks are never watered down on any night.

Once niggas start drinking, they become infatuated with all the hoes. I once caught a bad ass white girl, named Jenny Penny. She had a little height standing just above 5'9, long blonde hair, and she had some electric blue eyes. She was such an exceptional hoe and she had niggas literally going out of their minds. There's times this lil bitch would trick off like 12 to 13 niggas effortlessly in 1 day. What was her most fetching feature was her adorable double d breasts with full brown nipples. In kinky manners she was a pro in making niggas bust-off between her fluffy boobs and she knows how to work her feet. Skillfully she could grip a niggas pole and make him orgasm and one gentleman fall asleep. Blending Jenny Penny in with the other hoes, and it worked out well. In '09 when I got busted for dogfighting, and everyone was so shocked and couldn't believe it. However the old white judge magistry put a 180 k bail in order for me to get out. With out even having to dig in my stash Boitae wired the cash, to my bondsmen, and I was released later on that night. Now on the flip side, prior to me getting jammed up for this case, I had rented a club out for all of us to make money, turn up and have a good time, and also watch the super bowl. This was the year the New Orleans Saints played the Chicago Bears, eventually I did make it there to the event, but none of the hoes in nonchalant manners wouldn't let any of the men touch them. Once I showed up in the building instead the place erupted with gaily smiles and celebration times. As soon as I stepped foot in there the hoes placed a slew of flower necklaces around my neck plus I was showered with rolls and rolls and rolls of money, you know being that I had just arrived home.

While the night was still vivid, we all flew back to the spot, and the show really popped off. My twin bitches Bre and Ke (AKA Moody Girl), some high rollers wanted my hoes to perform, so we had to drive 45 minutes to Lincoln. Once we arrived there the set up was lavish. Once my girls hopped out and stepped in you should've seen the look on those niggas faces. I could see that automatically none of these guys had ever seen hoes so games and resplendent. Nevertheless once the festivity jumped off the twins started doing their thing. Which was, a simple text book way to hype the customers to throw some dollars, I grazed Kee (by the way I'm fucked Bre), on the ass hyping the moment. She caught a little fit but everything ended up working out for my stable. The party payed like they weighed, paying both girls $250.00 off top. Then they began to shake and bake. When we finally left my stripper's counted 2000 a piece.

Then I had a party at Boochie's poker game, food, liquor, and hoes. Of course there were plenty of people there. Duke was spending bank rolls of cash, Funk was there too, having a good time enjoying the moment, the entire neighborhood and surrounding hoods knew it was going down tonight. Making shit go bad Duke's shorty came in the spot and the two started brawling. Tearing up my damn place, so T-Hall (my bodyguard kicked their ass out), which didn't do any good because soon as that they kept going at it right in my front yard. I mean some real fatal attraction type of shit.

Moments later the police showed up. "Knock-knock-knock! Knock!" T-Hall answered the door once he saw 2 police officers he slammed the door dead in their faces. And in an instant the whole spot went into frantic mode running around recklessly. Crack, guns, scales, pills and all kinds of things were getting thrown out the windows, it was pure pandemonium. Somebody even tossed a fistful of powdered cocaine in the fish grease. I even took cover myself with all four pockets full I had to think quick. "Bang-bang-bang-bang!" "This is the police open up this door now!" Barked the angry cop, on the other side of the door. As for the aftermath the pigs cleared the spot, and thankfully they didn't lock anyone up.

Furthermore not even one hour later, we all come back to the spot like nothing ever happened.

# Shark Food

## Millennium Reedz

Walter and I were already back on our side of town. I noticed I had missed three calls on my burner. The call that caught my attention was from my cousin Pezo, who had also sent a text. "Call me ASAP!" When I hit his line up, he told me to "pull up ASAP." "Say less," was all I said. I was in route in seconds. You see, Pezo is my cousin from the South side of town and sure as shit stinks, it's real over there as well.

Once arriving, I was met outside by my other little cousin Mike Mike and Megee. I mean all of us have the same blood running through our veins.

"Yo, big cuz, we got the word that this pussy ass sucker was trying to line you up (hoodwink), and rob one of your gambling spots. Stupid ass buster ain't even know we was family.

"Oh, word," was all I said as fire boiled in my eyes. I knew this was serious business. The residence that I pulled up to was a-bando, with plastic coverings on the windows. The time was a little past seven in the evening and it was getting dim out. We stepped into the back room where there was a man with duct-taped feet and hands. He was on the floor, laying on his stomach, squirming. Pezo kicked the dude in his ass and told him to turn over. When the dude flipped over, I still couldn't see his face, because his nose was broken, and pushed off center. Blood soaked gauze protruded from each nostril. There was a gash over the right side of his head and his lower lip was cut in the middle. I say his eye was about to pop out of socket, that's what it looked like. There was blood leaking from his ear.

Then the dude looked at me and mumbled, "Py-Rex, it wasn't me."

Meege started laughing. "Oh, it wasn't you who called my phone."

He mocked the dude, " 'I got the drop on Big Boi Py-Rex and he is a cold pussy' and that you had to have him. Huh, sucker?" SLAP!

Instinctively, Meege smacked spit from the dude. Being more vigilant, I made out the dude's face and it was a fabricated, fake-ass hustler, want-to-be-pimp named Drake Shepard from over the south side of town. Back in the day, I used to have him under my wing. Over time, flaws and imperfections revealed and I realized he was faker than a three-dollar bill. I immediately cut him dry. Suspense filled the air followed by a few quiet seconds. Looking down at him, I started laughing, which made everybody else start laughing. Even the joker duct-taped on the floor shared a giggle. In diabolic fashion we laughed for another brief second and in that second, I knew his fate. Mike Mike asked me, "what do you want us to do with him Big Cuz?"

Poor Drake Shepard was watching the words come out of my mouth with the unswollen eye as I spoke. "Feed him to the sharks."

"No! No! No! Noooooo! Please Py-Rex, don't do me like that man! God!" "Fuck you snake," as I spit directly in the good eye. My cousins aggressively threw a blanket over him and started rolling him up, forcefully. He started hollering and kicking his legs vigorously. At that moment, my lil cousins don't look like the loving and caring little cousins I grew up with. They now look like dark deadly demons.

Down the ocean front, the home the ferocious sharks, there are 17–18-foot bull sharks that will chew him up in three of four bites and won't leave any evidence. There's plenty of times cops found body parts regurgitated on the beach sands, and they could never put a name with the gruesome remains.

I told my cousins to "hit the burnout"

when they take care of what's now shark food. "Say less Big Cuz," was all was said.

# Baltimore Love Story

## @Djay_amazin

"Get in line and hurry up. I'm not taking no ones and I'm not giving out no change. Ayo watch the corner while I hit these junkies before they come, we got the best dope in the city right now, junkies coming from all over the place. Shit I can put this dope on the moon and they're coming to get it no matter what. It's been a long morning we've been rocking since this morning just to keep the foot traffic down out of respect for the neighbors. Unc that lives at the corner house just did an interview with the Baltimore Sun Paper about the open air drug market that we got running on the block at the moment. Uncle Chuck keeps yelling out purple haze hitting in the hole and of course that nigga is late as usually he has been up all night chasing ready rock "crack". Knowing damn well we need him in the morning. Uncle Chuck's the type of junkie that swears to you up and down that he was the slickest nigga in his time, he would come outside with some old ass sweat pants on with some shorts over top of the sweat pants, some corn rows, one gold tooth in his mouth with the rest of his teeth gone with a stocking cap on his head made out of somebody's grandmother's stockings. Typically Baltimore shit you can't tell him shit once he get that smack "dope" in his system he wants to start dancing and cleaning up the whole block.

Back to business as usual daily trips to the corner store owned by the Muslim we keep running back and forth buying sunflower seeds and 25 cent bags of chips just to keep the Muslim's mouth shut about the junkies sitting out in front of the store while we're waiting to get some more dope you know Hersl and his boy's "the police" on the way to shake the block down, just to take our packs and hit us where it hurts at. A nigga can live with that instead of taking a trip down to bookings to deal with the bullshit. 24 hours to see the commissioner just to get a $100,000 bail, little do they know I got a homegirl named Kia that's a bail bondsmen to post the bond. She's fine as fuck!! Out of respect for the OG's that're from my block, I would have been pressed up on her a long time ago. See how my block is doing numbers and how much power I have gained over the time. Kia be shooting her shot at me every chance she gets, pretty as fuck body out of this world ass shaped like a prefect heart, you can tell she works out five times out of the week, and vegan to the core "no meat at all," maybe she would make an exception for me.

It's Sunday, you know the city is going to be turnt up down at select lounge the Ravens beat the Chiefs you know all of the big dogs going to get there, let's not forget all of the bad bitches, Alexx "the club owner" ain't letting nothing under a 7 in there, Alexx don't be playing that shit. Every section is sold out bottles everywhere at Djay_Amazin Aka Hoodfavoritedj got the club rocking with the latest trap music got people in there two stepping, bitches shaking their asses to that song called "Princess Diana" by Ice Spice Featuring Nicki Minaj. Them niggas met up down select amazin already had the table lit with bottles flowing and females chilling at the table with us. Amazin whispered in Moe Joe's ear like "dummy let's go out of the country to some where like St. Lucia you know that's one of the places where I can go and fuck around with these females, cause you know wifey ain't having that shit."

Amazin's wife was a bad brown skin female from Greenmount Ave., ass like a Georgia peach ,pretty teeth, beautiful smile, down to earth, stay at home mom. She loves Amazin to death, ain't no way she was letting me go by myself. As always she break down and let me go by myself. She know for sure, all of them bitches be on my line and all of them want a piece of Amazin and they can't wait to tell my woman that I was fucking around on her. They're dying to post some shit on the gram about me to drop some tea, just for some clout these days. They're kissing and telling if you're the lime light, they know you and your girls so they have one up on you. Amazin always stayed fresh to death even on an off day, shoe game out this world. Amazin had the plug some Puerto Rico dudes who keep some good dog food at any given moment it was never an off day. They can give out free dope everyday of the week, just to keep the block doing numbers.

Amazin was born and raised in northeast Baltimore with the heart of a lion aint no cross in his heart. He on the radio every Friday night setting the tone for the city and by the morning getting the junkies their dope before they go to work every time. He's on the radio he shouting out every hood in between D.C. and Baltimore. The phone the line ringing off the hook, can't nobody get through the request line to give their hood a shout-out.

Moe Joe shake my hand like we leaving in the morning fuck the price we jamming with the smack (dope), right now who going to stop us, damn sure aint these niggas or the Feds. Little did he know the Feds were already watching Amazin and they were on his line like crazy.

The next morning Amazin pulled up on the block in a 2020 Honda accord with 5% tinted windows, you can't see shit, he just came around the way to collect the money before getting on the plane to go out of the country. Phone ringing off the hook wifey keep calling his phone. Amazin keep sending the phone call to the voicemail. He says to himself "she know I'm out here shaking and moving, I ain't got no time to be fussing about some bullshit.

" Soon as I answer the phone the Feds start chasing Amazin through the city tearing the city blocks up by the grace of God, Amazin gets away, he winds up driving straight to the airport in the process, Amazin starts calling everybody to tell them to dump their phones to avoid being tracked down he also closed down the dope spots for the rest of the day because it was too hot to be shaking and moving. Next he hop on the flight and met Moe Joe in St. Lucia, where at nighttime you can see your feet in the water and the air is so fresh, beautiful females all over the place walking around half-naked, keep talking about hey poppy. That shit be having Amazin going crazy. I had to grab Moe Joe from the airport on the ride back to the private villa. Amazin started to tell Moe Joe about the chase that just happened before they got on the plane. How you got Moe Joe, Amazin's right hand man, slick ass nigga from west Baltimore, but was raised over on the east side, Greenmount Ave to be exact. Moe Joe kept a pretty as coupe riding around the city with the top down at any given moment. Not to mention bro always had a bad bitch by his side.

Moe Joe was 10 steps ahead of niggas and went legal and grabbed some trucks and ran the bag up and he wasn't looking back for shit. I think the Feds going to grab me when I get back from vacation. So let's live it up while we're here, everything on me fuck it that whole week we were living it up to the fullest, fucking the gram up with all type of videos. Back in Baltimore they started questioning the people who live next door from Amazin, they had a picture of Amazin showing the neighbors. Somebody had put them on point about where Amazin was eating at that morning at the yellow bowl on Greenmount Ave.

The Feds blitz the breakfast spot and grabbed Amazin they had five black Tahoe truck's outside with every street in a five block radius blocked off like he done killed someone.

The US Marshals took Amazin to the federal building and booked Amazin on drug trafficking charges for trafficking muti kilos of heroin. The judge told Amazin you're a danger to the community, Amazin had one of the best lawyers in Baltimore, his name is Ivan Bates, Ivan Bates objects to the judge's choice of words. Mr Bates gave the judge the run down about how Amazin is a pillar in his community the judge grants Amazin a bail as soon as he get to the supermax jail cell. He called Kia the bail bondman and told her to come get him out of jail.

So Amazin tried his hand and she took the bait. Next thing you know they were on the side of the highway with the emergency lights on.

They climb in the backseat of the car and he started kissing her mouth, rubbing on her breast playing with her clip and sucking on it like it was a rose. That got her going to a point they started fucking like crazy. Amazin got her bent over fucking her from the back, that high yellow ass clapping with every stroke til Amazin cum, who would ever thought this is how the story ends....

# Pledge Allegiance 2

## Millennium Reedz

**Bouns excerpt from PLEDGE ALLEGIANCE TO THE BAG**

Taking in the beautiful views of the city. It was a late spring morning, just half past eleven. The cloud cover had started to thin and streaks of light from the rising sun bounced off the distant peak. But there yet, the sun would pop back from those clouds very gracefully.

I'm on my way to Greenbrier to meet up with my counterfeit connect. He's the best in the business. It took me about 20 minutes or so to arrive at the Savannah Suited Hotel, right off the interstate behind Joe's Crab Shack. I pulled up to the hotel and parked in back. I walked through the entrance with it's two sets of electronic double doors. The lobby was immaculate, and there were people on MacBook's and Apple tablets drinking hot coffee and eating danishes. A splendid day to do business, I thought to myself. The connect, Rico, was waiting on my arrival, so as soon as I stepped to knock, the ninth floor door opened to a sweet, majestic smell of air smacking me dead in the face. Oh my God was my first thought as an Asian chick with long shiny, black hair, looking like a model, let me in. Attractive in a vulgar manner, she wore a pair of fitted tights with a { Maryland Monroe } crop top, designed by GMG apparel. The Saint Laurent heels and matching purse complimented her outfit substantially. Adding to the scene and making this a very royal, foreign experience was a mean looking Spanish female with big breasts and full lips. Her hair was dyed at the ends, making her alluringly beautiful. The Dolce & Gabana frames also embellished her ideal features.

    Before any words were ever spoken, I witness the Spanish shorty feed g-bands fastidiously through a calibrated money machine. From how this was playing out, I thought I was watching a movie, from the crisp sounds from the cash, to the fast counting of bills brought chilling goosebumps to my arms. I pledge allegiance to the bag, as I placed my right hand over my chest.

# Overnight Success

## Reggie West

It was a warm, late night, out in West Tampa FL. The skies were dark which the stares were shining bright.

Tae Beas I met him over at Gyro's on 50th and Broadway, I pulled up to get five C-230 Percs for the forty-five. Momentary, all of a sudden Black Sam called me, instaedly I put him on speaker phone, "A yo homie, I got a life changing lick," as he paused trying to properly say the right words, "I know for certain it's like 200K plus, but you need a car." I hung up anxiously. I made a phone call to Kane to arrange us to grab his girlfriend's grandmother's Dodge Charger. Kane is my right hand man, you see him you see me. Next thing I explained to Kane and that we needed to link.

Once we linked up, I calmly told him face to face about what the situation we had at hand, "we gotta Powerhouse lick, who has 20 bricks, 500 pigs (pounds of exotic weed), 200K in cash on deck. Black Sam turned me on too, "what we're waiting on?" asked Kane with malicious intentions.

After about 10 more minutes or so, Kane was all-on-board, with the mission. As we hopped in the Dodge, insteateous I slammed 2 percs to the face -off rip-. As I'm clenching a 45 Desert Eagle, Kane also has a 40 Cal with a dick (extendo clip). Kane was speeding on the E-way, doing 80 MPH non-stop. We're blasting the hottest drill rapper on the streets Coreed [no hooks]... With the money on my mind and percs kicking in, put a diabolical smile stretched across my face. Insteadly turnt me into a madman.

Minutes later, we're on MacDill next Hines Street, then we made the first left and the apartments were sitting right in front of us. Justice Homes, were the name of the apartments. They were a 2 story, tan and beige complex, with stairs that connected to the units. Apprehensively we waited all night and, He showed up later that night. While observing him he deliver his drugs in a Dodge Caravan. More so he likes to meet his plays (drug addicts), at the Target down the street in the plaza. There were times when we witnesses not just one customer at a time shopping singly, but there were times 6-7 niggas would pull-up to shop, patiently, which each play would purchase their drugs in orderly fashion, customers would hop in his SUV. The gorilla inside of me, wanted to jam 'em up now. My pockets were touching, but I just remained patient.

Now two days later when we pulled up in front of his apartments, the lick was outside sitting down on the curb, (just talking on his phone while getting a breath of fresh air).

"Fuck this, I'ma get 'em now!" I said in livid fashion, ready to get it popping. "Naw- naw- Reggie, the money ain't shit,"

Black Sam assumed me firmly. Nodding my head in conception. A few hours later, I went home and took a shower, things were all blurry, because all throughout the night I thought of violence and trying to figure out a way. The next day we were in a Buick Lesable and Black Sam trailed us in a Dodge Charger. Meanwhile as we pulled up, listening to NBA Young Boy, as I stand in light whispers with the DE in my hands.

Holding the gigantic gun like a veteran. The music was up blasting, zoning-out to the lyric's of the prolific rapper indeed. We were watching him through the rearview mirror, this nigga didn't even know we was finna down his ass. Then all of a sudden a car pulled up, to Jose, next he goes upstairs with a duffle bag in his hands, seconds later he comes out with a smaller duffel bag. We could only imagine what each bag contained, but I knew for sure that I had to shave 'em.

As the sun sets and the night falls, he's now sitting outside on the curb, then out of the blue, he takes his phone out and took a picture of our car, we couldn't believe it. "Damn that car looks out of place," were the words that came out, as I read his lips. Jose was eyeing our whip as he walked by.

We had 10% tints on our windows, so they couldn't see our faces. Meanwhile totally out of the blue Kane walks up to their spot and knocks on the door. Throwing off the moment of possible recognizement. Mid-way through the night, we hopped on his trail, we were on his bumper, like flies on shit. Following him north-ward across Bush Street, then he turnt off, as then next he jumped on the interstate.

So in audacious fashion, we rode straight to his apartments, as Kane did a buck-twenty down the two-way, pulling up and jumping out of the Buick. We looked militant as we ran up the stairs, with crow bar in hand. Forcefully we both bashed the door, insteateously as bolts burst off the door handles. The first thing we saw were mad black trash bags stacked, piled up in the middle of the floor. And they were all filled to the rims with straight cash, I've never seen anything as fascinating and cultivating in my life.

Without even thinking I picked up four bags and was finna to bounce, "nigga do you see all these pounds?" Insteadily, I started looking around for some more trash bags, to load the smoke up. In beguiling manners we bagged everything up, closing the door behind us jogging the load to the Buick. We all jumped in two cars and we were ghost. Once making it back, we were trying to figure out and do the numbers to our lick. Kane didn't want Black Sam to get the same cut as our take. "We can't do it like this Kane," I said to my right hand, keeping the situation all the way G. He's the one who gave us the sting meanwhile we at the spot now and Kane done cuff some bread and pigs -off the dribble- . After weighing what I said, he thought briefly. The car was quiet for a few moments before he spoke, "Ok-ok, everybody strip," Black Sam yelled to both of us wanting to make sure nobody pocketed any extra cash or such, for safety business propose's.... That's rule #1, never trust no nigga. Soon afterwards, a peculiar feeling came in the room. Then slowly Black Sam slips of his shirt and places his all black .40 Cal on the table. Next as Kane put his Army fatigue .40 Cal on the table, then pulled a bulk of cash out his pockets. "Nigga where you get those racks from?!" Now livid with the situation all together. As I'm shaking my head, "oh hell naw," insteadly Black Sam went out back and checked Kane's car, and sure as shit stinks, he came back with 10 pigs in total( in clear zip bags). As I hiss through my teeth cause I don't like how Kane played this. Ultimately, we ended up, busted down 300 K, 21 bricks, and 500 pounds.

Jose came home to see his shit gone and called Black Sam with urgency assisting he needed help. 10 minutes later, Black Sam and Kane went to meet up with Jose at Union Street on North Blvd Homes Apartments (aka Da projects) Being that it was pitch black dark outside, Jose was underhandly peeping Kane, giving him the sly eye, attempting to put his face into familiar, but with bigger things on his mind he pushed it to the back of his mind.

# Dear Cancer

## Tranquil Justice

Dear Cancer:

"With my hair I would be cool, now am lonely looking like a fool,
Am hairless crying for love, society has anymore interest in me,
And the pain hurts me to the core,
At night through love songs like a desperation storm,
My tears pour, I miss the recent beautiful joyful life,
Vacation in Paris shopping in Dior,
Cuddling in bed with my love like two lovely doves,
Whisper into each others ears while our hearts rhyming,
To the sound of the beats of love."

Live From the Trenches

Patrick was sitting inside of his living room when he read the heart touching post on Ismael's Facebook wall. Patrick read "Dear Cancer", not once or twice, but seven times. And each time Patrick read the post he felt an intense battle of guilt overwhelming his body.

As Patrick was uncomfortable shifting onto the black leather couch while running his fingers through his long dreads, for a moment he thought to himself, "why should I feel guilty about my own hair just because somebody else can't grow theirs?"

Patrick was furious with himself for logging onto Facebook at the wrong time, because he feels the post was directly talking to him. Patrick didn't really know that much about Ishmael. He was just a Facebook friend for all he cared, but for some reason the conscience of guilt running through Patrick's impulse from reading "Dear Cancer," was torturing his heart and inner thoughts at the same time.

"Jeez," Patrick sighed in deep desperation.

Patrick decided to linger on Ishmael's Facebook page a bit longer to find out more about this person, because they have been Facebook friends for a while, but Patrick had only observed things about nature and beautiful graphic designs on Ismael's Facebook wall, and not much else.

Patrick scrolled through Ismael's profile and found out that Ismael is an African-American female, born and raised in Brooklyn, NY. Patrick also observed that she earned a Master's Degree on Architecture, so that explains a lot about the graphic designs on her Facebook wall.

While Patrick was learning more about Ismael, instant current of electricity sent a shock wave buzzing through his body, and goosebumps immediately spiked up on his skin.

Five years before Ismael learned that she was diagnosed with cancer her last trip was to Rome, where she'd drawn a similar sketch of the Vatican, the world's biggest church. And Patrick reminisced being on some sort of similar trip, before him and his highschool sweetheart Chantal parted ways, but Chantal and Patrick's very last trip after Rome was Paris. Where she fainted inside of a Christian Dior store. Later when she woke up at the hospital. A French doctor delivered the worst news of her life, that she was diagnosed with stage two cancer. When Chantal desperately scanned around the hospital room, Patrick was no where in sight, and ever since the thought of his absence broke her spirit.

While Patrick shifted into Ismael's inbox, he feel a slight of compassionate sensation flow down through his body. He'd already made his mind up, that he will cut his dreads and donate them over to Ismael. But some how he wished it was for Chantal instead and hope this good deed would outweigh his past mistake for betraying her in Paris.

"Hi Ismael, this is Patrick your Facebook friend. Besides accepting your friend request on Facebook and liking each other's posts, we haven't really had a chance to communicate, but truly your post 'Dear Cancer', touched me very deeply. My ex-love Chantal was also diagnosed with cancer and I feel bad for betraying the love we had for each other and that I'm cutting my hair and hope to donate it to you. I pray God will forgive me for walking out on Chantal at her lowest. This is my contact number please reach out for an address when you read this message. I will be more than willing to drop this gift off at your address." : Patrick pressed send.

Patrick rose from the couch and walked over to the bathroom, he looked around for some scissors. "Whew, oh God" Patrick whined with regret as he glanced down at the scissors with desperation while looking at the mirror and running his fingers through the beautiful dreads he will miss forever. "Where a man can be perfect without hair, a woman won't feel natural being bald. You should live life with no regrets when good deeds are applied. That's how you get your blessings in full, don't allow any irrational or any selfishness perspective to be the magnet of your distraction," the inner voice spoke to Patrick.

Patrick brought the scissors to his head and as he cut his long dreads, they started to fall into the sink before him one by one. When he was done he neatly packed the hair into a small clean plastic bag, after doing so Patrick was in a deep daze in front of the mirror trying to puzzle together his true image.

"Who is this man?" he asked the mirror. The ladies probably wouldn't waste their time with or spare a second looking at him in this instant...Patrick thought to himself. And for the first time Patrick and the inner soul in him laughed at that thought. Because Patrick's image will would take a while to reshape back to his normal face.

With the bag in hand, he returned back in the living room for his iPhone, and to his surprise Patrick was very pleased to see that Ismael wasted no time to reply back to his text message on Facebook, but why didn't she call he thought?

"Hi Patrick, that is so kind and wonderful of you. I've been enjoying watching you for years now. I am your next door neighbor...Ismael."

The reply startled Patrick and took him by surprise. He wondered to himself "how could she possibly know so much about him, when he only knew so little about her, this is an odd coincidence."

Patrick threw a baseball cap over his head to cover his bald head, and stepped out of his house. He was now standing on his mysterious Facebook friend's porch and in fact their porch's are connected. Patrick knew the inside-out of the two stories brownstone house next to his house to a tee. The 'For Sale' sign was removed almost three years ago, but Patrick never once noticed any sign of anyone living at the house and neither did he bother to ever meet his new neighbor.

Patrick pushed his index finger on the bell. Ding! Dong! And the familiar face coming to the door was not what Patrick expected, a lump formed in Patrick's throat he was in deep shock, it was his long time high school sweetheart.

"Chantal?" there she was with her long natural, curly hair joyfully hanging down on her shoulders, she'd beat cancer.

# Scammerz With Hammerz

## Meezy

Pocohauntas just stepped out of the shower, a towel wrapped around her head, her 6 foot tall voluptuous curves complimented her light complexion and glowing skin. But who doesn't know her, will be fooled by her innocent baby face and her professional business demeanor.

Pocohauntas sashayed over to the queen sized bed, she picked up the couple of thousand dollars spreading across and inhaled through the crisp stacks of money joyfully to Pochauntas she counts each night as just another come up. But to most men having a goddess like Pocohauntas in their bed's seems like heaven on earth.

As Pocohauntas turned to smack the opened pack of condoms off the bed, the ringtone, "Princess Diana" by the rapper Ice Spice echoed through the speaker of her iPhone 12, letting her know there's another customer ready to trick their last on her.

Pocohauntas dived on the bed for the phone, the sight of her voluptuous naked body spread across the bed would make Jennifer Lopez want to go on retirement, because every single inch on her body screams Coca-Cola itself.

"How can I help you?" Pocohauntas answered the call.

"Is this Pocohauntas? I am F&N I saw your pictures on Skip the games, I'd like to take you for a spin."

"Are you 12? Because you sound immature."

"Ma I'm 29, and my shit touches the ground."

"I mean are you the police asshole!" she shouted with frustration.

"Oh...I thought you asked what was the size of my dick," F&N joked.

"Ha-ha very funny," Pochauntas mimicked with sarcasm. "Anyways how many hours are we talking about?"

"A hour or two."

"I hope you know that will cost you right?"

"If I can't afford it I don't sweat it, just hurry up and bring your little pretty ass down there, I am outside," F&N challenged back with confidence.

"Outside? I thought your ass would be at my door step by now because I was not planning on stepping out for the night."

"Yo ma, I don't know anything about your private life and I hate surprises, but since I am digging your style I will throw you a couple of grand extra for the trouble," F&N proposed to her.

"Sounds just fine with me, I will be outside in 5," she asssured before their lines disconnected.

Up front Pochauntas building, F&N lays back in his Maserati truck with suede seats, the street lights shining through his car window plays a radiant spark in his jewelries.

As F&N checked himself in the mirror, the ringtone "Intense" by the rapper Money Man echoed through his phone.

"Yo Swipe, what's the deal?" F&N answered on the first ring.

"I know you ain't ready for another 100 G swiping spree again tonight, bruh I'm half milli up, I'm finna treat myself with a bad bitch," he continues to brag.

"Shit money, don't sleep why should we, these hoes can come after."

"Look whose speaking lover boy ass nigga," F&N joked.

"At least I aint the one married," Swipe shot back.

"Anyway peep game, Meech just dropped of 2,000 Panda cards that's enough to put a lot of money on the board right now, I already purchased two first class tickets to Cali, what you say?"

"What do I say? Shit...We gonna celebrate, I'ma swing by your crib I gotta reward for you, I'ma let you have fun with this one like you said

I'm just gone chill with wifey, she been tripping lately."

"Shit...Seems like you wear your sleeves on this one, I never heard you talk with this much sympathy about Samantha since yall been married," Swipe joked.

"Whatever nigga ain't nothing change but a little piece of paper that doesn't mean I gotta be committed to that."

"Aight nigga just hit me when you outside," Swipe said before their lines went dead.

"Damn where the fuck is this b...." F&N's breath got cut short when he spotted Pochauntas' shapely voluptuous self modeling towards his Maserati truck. She wore high heels and a sun dress that complimented every single curve on her body, her long curly hair hanging to her shoulders.

F&N bumped his horn, to grab her attention, her hazel eyes sparked on the truck like a 12 o'clock brighten stars. As she walked over to the passenger side, F&N leans over and pushes the door open for her.

"You're such a gentleman, thank you," she complimented as she jumped in the seat.

With lust and admiration in F&N's eyes, he examined every single inch on her exotic goddess body.

"I swear you could of fooled me if we'd met on any other circumstance."

"And why you say that?" Pochauntas asked as she did a once over examining F&N's boyish swagger and liked what she saw.

"You look like you could be a lawyer or an actress why did you choose this lifestyle?"

"Are you judging me?"

"I don't mean any harm ma, my bad."

Pochauntas did a once over examining the polished car. "Is this car yours?"

"Like I said if I cant afford it, I don't sweat it."

"Are you a drug dealer or something?"

"I don't play about drugs ma, I lost my mom from an overdose," F&N scowled.

"Sorry to hear that," she sighed, for a long hot second the silence got thick in the air until the ringtone came through the speaker phone.

The phone was sitting in the cup holder, when Pochauntas glanced at the screen the word 'wifey' popped up. "Are you going to pick that up?" she challenged with a slight attitude.

"Why you sound like you're in your feeling, you aint my girl."

"I chase money, I don't chase dick nor pleasure."

"Why your heart so cold? You never thought of someone scooping you off your feet one day?"

"I don't sweat no relationship."

"And why?"

"For shit like that," she nodded over F&N's phone going off again and again. "I can't trust no man."

"Likewise I don't trust no bitch, who said she hasn't just sucked another nigga's dick."

"Then that's your fault, she ain't asked to be wifey, how can you judge her?"

For the rest of the ride F&N and Pochauntas rode to Swipe's crib in silence, once he hit Pacific Avenue at Virginia Beach, F&N pulled up into a four car garage spot mansion and parked.

The glamorous view of the luxurious atmosphere was like a breath of fresh air to Pochauntas she never saw anything like this. "Whose house is this?" she asked.

"A sibling," F&N pulled out his cell phone and dialed a single digit.

"As beautiful as this mansion is let me guess, that's where you take your female guests when you wanna trap their hearts."

"If that's what you wanna call it, but I ain't looking to impress anybody. That's just my everyday life style ma," F&N stepped out of the car with the phone glued to his ear. "Open the door," F&N requested on the phone without giving Swipe a chance to say a word.

Pochauntas followed behind F&N as she admired the beautiful house in awe.

Once they stepped foot inside the house Pochauntas was in a deep trance of admiration. The large spaced out place was painted all white with long spiral stairs, all white suede couch sitting on the living room with 70" Apple flat screen tv hanging on the wall with theater sound speakers and pictures of Scarface hanging 10 feet above the tv.. Somewhere from a perfect angle

Pochauntas could make out a MSR - Magnetic strip reader, embosser, fake drivers licenses, high definition magnetic printer, and Apple laptop with numerous different colored passports including crisp stacks of hundred dollar bills on a desk.

Out of nowhere Swipe appears in the living room drinking straight out from a bottle of Ace of Spades, he stood 5'9" tall with brown complexion, black curly fashion dreads that hung to his shoulders, and chinky eyes that attracted the ladies.

"Hi I'm Swipe," he introduced himself snapping Pochauntas out of her trance.

"I figured that," she nodded toward all the scamming equipment on the living room desk. "I am Pochauntas," she shook his hand.

"Yeah," Swipe glanced over his shoulder at the desk.

"What do you know about this field?"

"Since the bank gave us some hard time clearing them checks, I guess credit cards and gift cards haven't been so disappointing after all," she challenged.

"Wow, I am impressed, maybe you should fly out to Cali with us, an extra hand would be great, what do you say F&N?" Swipe suggested but in a more offering tone. F&N hasn't had a chance to answer, his phone hysterically ringing, going off again, when he checked, he saw 'wifey' popped up on the screen.

"Since I see you two done sparked some sort of chemistry I'ma just leave you two alone," F&N offered.

"Wifey must got you wrapped up by the balls, tell her I send my love," Pochauntas shot sarcastically.

"Whatever," F&N shooed Pochauntas, "just don't have too much fun, be ready tomorrow," he warned swipe before rushing out of the house, on his way to the car F&N finally answered his wife call.

"Nigga where the fuck have you been, I've been calling your phone for dear life," the female voice boomed through the speaker all hostile.

"Samantha you better watch your tone when you speak to me, because I didn't send you to college to be this ratchet," F&N said backing up from the driveway with such speed that he hadn't noticed the police car driving up the street behind him.

Inside the police car are two pale police officers that look more like KKK members than two civilians doing good deeds for the country.

The police driver swiftly cut his siren on.. SKRR!!

F&N swiftly pumped on the brakes, "please pull your car over on the side of the road sir," the police on the passenger seat shouted through the speaker.

"Shit," F&N hissed.

"What was that?" Samantha asked, curious.

"Bae, I will call you back."

"You know what, fuck you, I am through with this always remember what goes around will come back around, you wanna go have fun with your little hoes go ahead and be my guest," she rattled under her tongue.

"Aight you know what, since you want to know what's going on, go ahead stay," F&N shot furiously and put the phone on speaker.

Both police officers step out of their cruiser with hands rested on their gun holsters as they approach F&N's ride.

The office on the driver side tap the window with his flashlight, he rolled down the window.

"Can you tell me where you were speeding to?" he stared down at F&N with pure hatred.

"Does this ride belong to you young man?" the other police asked, his eyes beamed around the ride with admiration.

"Nah."

"Nah? This car is stolen?"

"Nah I bought it for my wife as a gift, for graduating college."

"And how old are you?"

"29."

"29? What are you some sort of gangsta rapper or something or a scammer?" the officer standing on the passenger side asked, noticing the expensive jewelry on F&N.

"I am neither," he replied back with this sarcastic smirk.

"You know what, I have had enough of your shit, show me your drivers license and registration," the officer standing on the driver side with a bit of frustration.

Meanwhile Samantha had been on the phone quiet this whole time, while Swipe was disturbed by the effect of the bright cop lights lighting up the place. Him and Pochauntas had been hiding behind a curtain window, observing everything.

F&N leans over and opens the glove compartment, the Glock he usually carries was near the edge of the door, it slips and falls on the floor, both officers waste no time and went to panic mode, they both pull the weapons and point it at F&N.

"Fuck this nigger's reaching for a gun," they both yelled in unison.

"I have a license......" BOOM! BOOM!

Samantha screamed on the speaker phone, for the first time the officers realized F&N may have them on record, but meanwhile they haven't also noticed Swipe and Pochauntas hiding somewhere behind the house window observing everything.

Swipe dropped to his knees, he couldn't believe the person he loves the most on earth just died before his eyes.

"God," Swipe sobbed, "F&N was more than a cousin to me." Tears were streaming down his face, "he was more like a brother to me, that was everything these racist cops just took away from me, my partner in crime."

Pochauntas placed a hand on Swipe's shoulder, "don't worry you got me now, and I promise I will never leave your side," she assured. From then on Swipe and Pochauntas would be one of the strongest scamming teams the world was not ready to face, because their credit card game was so strong, they loot every single brand stores like the mad waves of a storm.

# The Realest Ever

## Millennium Reedz

The streets of Jacksonville weren't shit to play with. I've been running those motherfuckers since almost 14 years old. Years later, now I'm running the underworld like Harriet Tubman, I've been running my whole hood [ Carevon Projects ]. I'm not a gang banger, but there's plenty of Cutthroat Committee running around down here. You see, I'm a paper chaser, if it don't make dollars it don't make sense. I'll turn form 0 to 100 real quick for my currency.

Now opposite to the fact, there were plenty of times when weak niggas turned to me to handle their beefs. I really didn't mind. My static is preeminent and my word is always bond. If I gave somebody I fuck with my word, keenly that meant, it would get handled.

That was then, this is the past. Now today was a new chapter, I excluded myself from any madness, or frivolous activity. At the end of the day, I knew shit can get extremely real, extremely quick. I've seen over 20 niggas, (just from my project), get their nose wiped! So in fact as I knew of, I didn't have any beefs with any niggas around the city. Needless to say my homies Takeoff and Piraranna, I wasn't so sure. They were involved in all kinds of illegal jobs and making bands by any means necessary.

Quiet as kept BBG (which stands for Born Go Getter), is what you called a one-stop shop. He stood, just over 5'4, brown skin, bald head, with an ambush of tattoos, from the neck down that was conspicuous to the eye. The ladies joked and teased him saying he resembled a short version of Tracey Morgan, but his muscular physique is chiseled. Seemingly even though his schedule gets busy he diligently stays committed to the work out. Monday - Friday, meaningful he wakes up at 5:15 am to get adequate -burn time- work out in. In his mind, that plays efficient to his longevity, productivity, and decision making.

Furthermore, as he stepped out of the apartment he was like always in chic fashion, he was in fact dripping in the latest designer-type. The Ferragamo spike toe sneakers, left sprinkles on the floor from the drip. More to add, his Dior fitted jeans were on fleet, along with a hitters edition GMG apparel button down. Even his watch was branded by the sensational designer Tom Ford.Fourty minutes later, In colorful posture Jenn jumped seemingly in his arms, met by a soft kiss. With hands palming her voluptuous butt cheeks, insteadily gave him a simi.... The two started dating recently and he was still trying to figure her out. However next, he spoke to Breonna "what's popping Bre," making her blush. "Hey BGG what's been going on?" Jenny asked just making light conversation.

Re-filing her glass, taking two gulps, "it's trying to pick up," he said while illustrating with empathis with his hands. "But I can't complain, I met you right?" as his question was clearly a statement.

Giving him a small punch in his stomach. "BGG I think you're the one," Jenny admitted veracious as ever. Placing a wet kiss dead center on his full lips. "ALLLLL yall two look cute together," Breonna added.

As a little time passed by, killing the elephant in the room, Jenny asked, "do you have any ecstasy?" Unfortunately he was out of that, what-so-every, but he said "he had the next best thing." As the girls sat inquisitive in their seats listening to his every word with total anticipation. Underhandedly digging into his Champion book bag pulling out a small baggie of what looked like lucid glass, "you know I keep the exclusive party-pack right?" he asked, knowing damn well the answer. "This is Molly," he said with emphasis, but the girls didn't have a clue. "Oh....I heard of that stuff," Jenny said with a giggle.

Fascinated by what looked like dazzling chips off a crystal. "It's an upper or a downer?" Breonna asked uncannily still amazed at what she saw. "It's an upper," he said. A few moments of silence pasted by before either one of them responded, "well let's do a blast," Jenn said blushing greatly which came from out of nowhere. Using the bottom end of his lighter, he crushed 5-6 crystals up into a dollar bill, next afterwards he took out his driver's license and refined the almost dust Molly into powder substance. Next, he used his pinkie finger, dipping it into the white-ish pink molly and inserted the potent drug underneath his tongue. "It's boot-up time," in alacrity postures he said.

Beckoning for Jenny to hand him her drink to wash it down. Grimacing was the expression on his face. Momentary after a few seconds of procrastinating and sure as shit stinks, the girls followed suit. Afterwards in revel fashion Jenny cut on the Bluetooth and the party was on.

# Super Grimmie

## Millennium Reedz

On the Southside of town, they've been parked in front of a two-unit brick apartment, just observing the scenery. It was a warm evening with the sun dropping behind the clouds, turning the sky pink and purple. A, Lil Rick, Moonie, and Hot Rod sat in the rental car puffing on a cigarette they deliberated strategically on the jooks." Damn. You see how many people are coming and going from out this dudes' spot?" Hot Rod sarcastically said.

"Yeah, the dude White Bread's crib is doing numbers," Moonie said, nodding his head. The intended lick, White Bread had so much traffic coming in and going out, it left three separate dirt paths leading to and from the front door. A couple of empty forty-ounce bottles in the yard confirmed that it was some live wires occupying the unit. White Bread was an older hustler in his late 30's. Tall, slim, a high yellow bone with long calm rolls, he had made himself a marked man when he and his crew went into RC's strip club. He threw about twenty bands on strippers alone, not to mention the AP bust down watch he wears around Shark City. That's like 50 racks price tag, easy.

"We'll never catch a dull moment at the rate this spot is booming. We gotta do Plan B," Hot Rod said in beguiling fashion. In quick succession, Hot Rod got out of the car and fixed his shirt to fully cover the Springfield forty Cal he had tucked on him. "Imma cop some smoke from dude and yall come knock at the door in five minutes sharp," Hot Rod barked before shutting the passenger door. "Say less, Bro, we're on it," Lil Rick said, locking eyes with Moonie.

As Moonie and Lil Rick watched, Hot Rod looked to the left and then looked to the right before crossing the street. He looked cool and calm as he walked to the unit with shameless boldness, knocked a couple times. Moments later, he disappeared into the spot.

Waiting patiently in the car, Moonie and Lil Rick made all the last-minute adjustments. Three minutes later, without any words being said, in effrontery gestures, they walked up to the crib. Knock-Knock-Knock. A few seconds later a brown skinned dude wearing a Strong edition GMG all-cotton round neck shirt with a matching Louis Vuitton strap back opened the door. Instantly the sweet smell of sour Diesel hit their nostrils. They didn't see any kids. They didn't see any dogs. Without any posturing or delay, they stepped into the apartment.

# Escaping Death 2

## Tranquil Justice

Sandra's face was overwhelmed with fear, one side of the sheet was folded upwards, which uncovered the burnt missing part of the dead corpse's face. All Sandra saw were bones and burnt skin with threatening long sharp teeth. The corpse's eyeball was wide open.

"AAAH!" Sandra screamed in horror, causing Renette to also jump in terror.

"Sandra enough!" Renette shouted because she was being interrupted from doing her job.

"Come sink your behind here into this chair," she said pointing to a black cushion wheeled chair.

"Mom how much longer do we have to be here? I can't take this anymore."

"We would have been long gone already if it was not for your scared self that kept dragging me behind from my job," Renette was now exhausted and irritated from Sandra.

Sandra sluggishly dropped into her seat by now the salt had her feeling thirsty she started whirling around from her seat for the spring water bottle, it was no where in sight.

"Mom have you seen my water bottle."

Renette also went for a quick glimpse, "it should be somewhere in the mop closet," Renette said, when the bottle was no where around in their view. But Renette already know it was a done deal, because there was no way Sandra would walk back in there herself.

To Renette's surprise, Sandra proved her wrong, she got up from her seat, first she walked over to the burning dead corpse's face that had her scared. She fixed the sheet to how it was supposed to be fixed over the body, then Sandra picked up the wet floor sign and clamped it down to where she'd just cleaned up her mess.

Renette was in awe when she watched her once scared daughter wheel the mop bucket back to the mob closet, when Sandra got there sure enough her spring water bottle was standing on the cleaning supplies themself, but before reaching for it Sandra figured she'd empty out the dirty waste water out from the bucket and also clean up the mop before hanging them up.

While doing so, the light blinked on and off, Sandra was a bit frenetic. But then thought it was probably her mom fooling around to scare her. So she went on to finish cleaning up the mop bucket along with the mop, and placed them where they belonged.

Sandra washed her hands clean then reached for her water bottle, the light blinked on and off again, "uh," she gasped.

In horror she shook, from her fears when the light was back on. Sandra exhaled hard on her way out of the mop closet, because she didn't know what to expect when she walked out there to the dead corpse.

"Mom," she called out on her way out of the mop closet, Renette didn't respond.

"Mom," again no answer, Sandra started to speed her up pace. She sighed in relief when she saw Renette was too busy focusing on stitching Belinda's body back together.

"I would gladly appreciate it if you would stop annoying my ass, so I can finish doing my job."

"Cool," Sandra agree, she flopped onto the chair.

"Why was the light blinking?" she asked.

"It must be pouring outside."

"Oh." They both were quiet for a long time, Renette peeked over to where Sandra was at, she was asleep. Within instants Sandra woke back up from feeling someone's hand playing with her long curly hair.

"Mom are you ready to go now?" Sandra yawned, she heard nothing but the hand was still playing with her hair. Sandra whirled the chair around to find a dead corpse with a missing head in front of her.

"AAAH!" she screamed and took off running, Renette was laughing.

"Honey, please stop I was only joking."

"I hate you," Sandra screamed back and continue running for the door, how did Sandra find her way out of the Guarino basement to the main street? She didn't know.

It was dark outside, and raining hard in her right state of mind. She rushed through the streets.

SKRRR SCRURR! Car tires are crying from drivers pushing hard on their brakes.

"Sandra!" Renette screamed.

Early morning at sunrise, before leaving home for work, she stopped by her daughter's bedroom, Renette admired her sleeping angelic face, in her hand was the notepad she was taking notes from the dead corpse's clipboard.

"What if she's have died last night?" Renette thought, she vowed to never play with her ever again.

"Love you angel," Renette said, planting a kiss on Sandra's forehead, before she left her home to begin her investigations on Belinda's death.

Renette's first interview was with this six foot tall heavy set chubby white complexioned female with short black hair above her neck, her weight was perfectly complimenting her size, her name was Gloria and she was Belinda's best friend. Gloria had this pretty glowing face, with the prettiest innocent smile that could warm up a serial killer's stone cold heart.

Renette learned from Gloria that, she and Belinda were co-workers for a Crypto stock market. On the weekend Belinda would do a little modeling for Victoria Secret.

"Um Gloria, do you mind if I ask you again, how close you and Belinda were?"

"Wow, we shared a sister-hood bond."

"Are you a married woman Gloria?"

"Oh God no."

Gloria broke out in tears, Renette wasn't sure why, she was a bit confused because throughout the interview, for a best friend, Gloria hadn't showed Renette any signs of emotion or sorrow towards Belinda's death.

"Okay, Gloria, I am sorry for your friends death, have a good day."

Renette left Gloria alone, so she could continue on her investigation, before heading to interview Belinda's husband named Johnny. The next few witnesses Renette interviewed after Gloria had already warned her a few things about Gloria that she'd kept secret from Renette.

First Gloria lied about her marriage with Daniel, and also she'd failed to let Renette know that her husband Daniel was also her best friend Belinda's personal body trainer.

And the next witness told Renette that weeks before Belinda's death, it was whispered around town that Belinda and Daniel were more like a couple instead of gym partners.

And Johnny, Belinda's husband didn't seem to care much about the disturbing heart breaking news, as long as she was happy to be enjoying living under his roof, Johnny loved it. Because he'd always say that, he was lucky to be with a stern exotic blonde like Belinda.

Johnny was this 5 foot tall white complexion looking nerd that females like Belinda would take advantage of. But with Belinda things were different, she treated Johnny with care and love, but people think that because Johnny had a lot of money, he owned one percent share of the Crypto stock market.

"How about their sex life?" Renette would ask.

"Ugh, terrible," most female witnesses would shoot back at Renette. Which she can see possible about why Johnny would be okay with Belinda flirting around with other men. Often men could be tender hearted and head over heels with a female for the wrong reason, sometimes it may not be because they are in love with that female, but love her exotic shapes and goddess looks.

When Renette got to Johnny's house to interview him, her face was frowned with deception. When she spotted Johnny sending away this beautiful brunette female with some kisses to the forehead. She was tall with a stern body of an athlete, and Renette'd guess she probably would say a basketball or soccer player.

"Johnny?" Renette's voice sounded hurt as if she could feel for Belinda, because she was also a woman.

"This nerd must be attracted to exotic women only," Renette thought.

"And Becky please drive home safe, please remind your dad to contact me it's important," Johnny yelled after the beautiful brunette, who was just getting into the passenger seat of a two door low rider covert race car.

Becky didn't answer Johnny she simply gave him the thumb.

On the driver side was this Asian complexion gentleman with red colored dragon tattoos running across his left arm.

"Take care Johnny," he yelled.

"Alright Lee, be good with my niece now," Renette was relieved when Becky was also a relative.

Vroom! Vroom! Vroom! Lee stomped his foot down on the gas, dark clouds of smoke spit out from the muffler. Renette and Johnny had their nostrils covered in-between coughs.

"Ugh! Can't trust him being around my niece, not one bit," Johnny snarled in disgust.

Johnny was finally caught off guard by the beautiful light complexion beauty before him, when he turned to look in her direction.

"I am sorry ma'am, how can I help you?" he asked politely.

"I am with Life After Death insurance company, and I have a few questions for you, concerning your wife's death."

Johnny stepped inside welcoming Renette into his apartment.

"Belinda and I were only fiances, we were supposed to be married sometime around December 25th, that's what I've always wanted for Christmas, a beautiful angelic snow flake like Belinda to be my wife."

"An autopsy did run on her and rat poison was found in her food," Renette revealed. "Do you know anything about that?"

"How come?" Johnny broke into tears, "she was just too nice and friendly to everyone, that's impossible."

"Do you know anything about her involvement with Daniel, Gloria's husband?"

"This evil brat," Johnny snarled.

"Did you know that's her fourth husband? And I'm praying Daniel gets her before she gets him."

Renette was no rookie to know what Johnny was referring to.

"Gloria's my sister," Johnny revealed. "Becky was her daughter."

"Is Becky also Daniel's daughter?"

"No."

"She is the daughter of Gloria's first husband."

"Supposedly he was dead, but how was he going to contact you if he's dead," Renette recalled Johnny's request to Becky earlier.

"Right my sister is very strict every man she start fooling around with, she'd also made Becky believe that they're all her father."

"Why is it so important that you're so desperate to get in touch with Daniel if he was screwing your fiance?"

"He offered to contribute to Belinda's funeral."

"Have a nice day Johnny, sorry about your fiance."

Renette had heard enough, sometimes to solve some mystery like this. You must go back to square one and Belinda's best friend Gloria seem to be the prime suspect in her murder.

Meanwhile Sandra had the little black notepad monitoring her life around, anything on the notepad that had something to do with how those corpses at Guarino morgue died, Sandra was not doing.

She was scared to drive, afraid that she would die in a crash. She was scared to eat, afraid that she would be poisoned. She was in deep misery, Sandra couldn't bear torturing herself leaving her life like this, her anxiety started kicking.

Meanwhile before Renette went home, she stopped at a florist shop and bought Sandra some flowers and an apology card for what had happened last night to her over at Guarino.

When Renette reached home it was already 4 in the afternoon, she knew Sandra should be back home from school a few hours from then.

"Sandra," she called out, not getting an answer.

"Sandra," again no answer, and that's not like her daughter, usually loud music would be flowing from her bedroom speakers. When Renette rushed to Sandra's room it was empty.

"Sandra, baby," she called out now checking the bathroom area.

AAAH! Renette screamed, "No, my baby!"

She broke down in tears, Sandra was laying in a bloody pool in the bathtub, on top of the tub was a sharp razor blade and her wrist was next to the blade pouring red.

"No, no, no, please baby wake up," Renette's voice cracked into a soft whisper, she rushed over to Sandra's side, cupping her beautiful angelic face.

"Baby please come back, mommy loves you."

Boo! The sudden sneer startled Renette, she swiftly pushed Sandra away from her, back peddling.

"Gotcha," Sandra chimed. "It's only red wine mom, I had to get you back for what you did to me last night."

A sudden spark of electric shocking pain, ran through Renette's body and hit her heart, her body starting to shake violently, before it collapsed on the bathroom floor.

And this time Renette's soul hoped Sandra didn't think that, her corpse stretching on the bathroom isn't a prank.

Renette will never get to solve Belinda's murder case, and Renette will be this perfect friendly ghost Sandra will forever have to live with because the house will be forever haunted with Renette's blood and spirit forever.

# Trap

My nickname T.R.A.P.P. stands for: "To rip any parts possible", this isn't just a name, it's a title. For the ladies Tavaris Ramsey as pussy pleaser. Well my mother calls me weasel, nasty and Mr. Go. All these names, I earned them. One night I ran up my hoes, we had a party over at my first wife Fee's, sister's Tammy's house. As soon as the music turnt on, we started doing our thing. I mean, not even 30 minutes into the show and the police bust the door in. Unbelievable they kicked in my other crib simultaneously. And once again, all sorts of illegal substances were tossed and thrown all over their place. In cunnly gestures, on someone attempted to hide a loaded 45 in the Captain Crunch cereal box.

As the -12- (police) didn't have any remorse whatsoever, as they had an ol- head (with 8 fingers), pinned spread eagle on the wall. To make matters somewhat more awkward the old man had a hot fish sandwich in his hand, then out of total terror for the cops he pissed on himself. Next afterwards we were all taken to jail, and put in the tank for hours. The county jail was so packed they placed men and women in the same bullpen.

Loren, was one of my special delights. When I first cut into her, she pulled up on me inquiring that she wanted to be a working girl. From Big Chic to sucking and fucking big dick. Now before I can officially add her to my hoe catalogue, first I had to break her in. She was very receptive to the fact and was willing to prove her diligence in the situation. Moments later, she stepped up close up to me, acting far from shy, seconds later she gently puled out my sausage out of my Nike sweatpants I had on. As she's sucking my dick, being undaunted I filmed the whole episode with my phone. Rule #3, never be shy for the camera like a proficient head hunter, she did tricks with her tongue and the saliva.

After about 20 minutes or so of straight unadulterated oral, I waved my crew into the room and each person took turns stroking her down one by one the entire time, while she never took her mouth off of the mic. I named her Doorbell cause she took the ding and dong, and she passed the initiation.

Another hoe I had's name was Tiffany (D. Hall babymother) and she wanted to be a star. At the time she was fucking with Mark Coleman. Tiffany has a wonderful personality, she had a butter pecan complexion. Her smile was breathe taking plus her teeth were pearly white and the most impeccable of them all. Let the truth be told, shorty was swole, but not too swole. So I asked her are you ready to get down and dirty for these bands. Her response was like Eddie Murphy, "I'll do whatever you want," I need you to be able to suck the perfect dick. Her response was, "can I show you what I got?" In uncandid gestures, "I guess," I said as even my eyebrows on to the top of my forehead.

Wearing what appeared to be a comfortable looking sundress she unslid the shoulder straps, causing the garment to fall completely down, unabashed with a gazed stare of focuses in her eyes, next she fumbled with my penis, kissing it as she grabbed it out of my Puma shorts. The two piece leopard ligr aroused me excitingly as she performed her magic. Next Tiffany licked and sucked and twisted her tongue on while looking me naughtily in my eyes. From the wet galvanizing feeling it literally made my mouth watery. Her eyes were majestic, they were pick-a-niece, mixed Alaska Husket.

Skillfully with no hands she came up slow, twisting and gripping her hands, like a biker boy with-in minutes, I started jerking like a robot. This is the top I even had I thought in delightment, but surely I couldn't let her know, so her name was made and earned then and there, Crack, cause I know I wanted more.

Trapp, I've been with over 100 hoes, I got hoes like Van Camp got beans.

I had another time, when we had to break in Snowflake, she came to the orientation. I tell her to take care of Boochie ( know Boochie's packing heavy) besides he's a B-Mo Bandit. I'm telling myself Boochie bout to kill this little white bitch. As she walks into the bedroom minutes later I heard loud moans and faint sounds of skin slapping aggressively. After about 15-20 minutes I step in the room to see Boochie sitting down in a chair, sweating bullets, while Snowflake laid across the bed provacativly, "I think she has still got a lil fight in her," he said half smiling. I waited briefly for a moment before I spoke, "ok- let me give you a call in a couple of days."

One night we're about to do a show in the club, all the hoes put the word out is what I tell them. As I'm walking through the club the DJ played my track, yall know why Trap aint scared, Trapp got bread, Trapp got the hoes that's ready to give head. The verse catch me riding through the rooftop, swirfen with the deuce cock, drinking shine and blowing mid, when I'm done I do-wop, I party like an animal/ stay hype like this my last day/ get up out the bid like a roach in my ashtray/ people say I'm nasty the way I have that broad to trick/ licking ass and suckin tits/ eating what cum up out my dick/ stun man it wouldn't be right if I didn't. I had times I was getting my dick sucked sitting down shitting. The first time it happened it was a shock, now it be my usual keep the broads hunting for me, like I be's a fugatave, stun man even when I have that softball, I'm south paw, I make it float like a golfball. When I bring my hoes to the club, I get 'em in at half price. All the girls in the strip club, they don't like when I come, because I get my homeboys not to throw no money at the hoes, because when they come to my spot they get wet pussy and sensational head for a good price.

# Terror On Line 1

## Millennium Reedz

The telephone rang, she knew she was going to die. The annoy in the moment was totally real, in real time. But nonetheless, she knew it with such certainty that she froze with a razor in her hands motionless. As the warm bath water now seemed hotter. Her body feeling panic insteady. Her hair stuck to the side of her face by the steams from the hot water. Even the bubbles in the bubble bath had seemed to dissolve. The water drops condensed on the top of the shower stall, onto the faucet, and furthermore onto the mirror. Even the floor had a light mist, but still constantly her telephone rang repetitiously. Ring-----Ring------Ring-----then a vibrate would follow, hummmmm---hummmmm-

hummmmm. As she could feel the vibrations from afar. The entire house was so quiet that you could hear a mouse piss. In a horrify manner she stayed scared still, holding her breath immediately, as though silence would change the predicament of her fate.

It was Tuesday settling late in the evening she was in a hot tub shaving her legs, arms, and all of the other private parts, a woman takes care of. She was very meticulous, and took pride in keeping herself up, with adequacy. Since a child she would always brush her teeth after every meal, even after playing outside she would wash her hands once coming inside the house. Ring----Ring-----Ring----Ring---hummm----hummmm---hummmm. Letting the call go unanswered it was 8:17 PM on a Tuesday night. The weather called for it to rain, but really there were light showers. How could it be, how in the world could anybody contact her flip phone burnout when she never gave out the line? How in the world could anybody call, when she just only brought the untraceable cellular flip phone from Wal-Mart just the day before. And just after she brought it, she only took the cellphone out of the plastic, set-up the settings, and hasn't called a soul.

It's clearly not a coincidence that this phone is ringing tonight. You see for years, Rolanda has been getting the same exact call, at the same exact time 8:15 PM sharp, up until just two weeks ago. Ingeniously, she's been working for the eminent Sinilower Cartel, as a transporter from state to state, a true road runner, and a paper chaser. Her credentials were impeccable and she never lost a load. That was until last week, when she decided to borrow a 100K without getting the ok. Rolanda had plans only to borrow the 100K and brick of Mexican mud, to make a quick move to buy some counterfeit that were the most guileful bills of them yet. The hollow grams look like they were printed straight out of the US monument. But they weren't. They were made from Beyji China. R-r-r-r-ring-- R-r-r-r-ring.

Mind boggling as it sounds but what confirms is just her luck had run out. Did they know where she lived? Did they know my moves? Did they know that she was here? Were the questions that were running through Rolanda's mind. As the minutes pasted on she wondered , maybe there would be a bad day for her after all, or would it? Then out of nowhere, she realized that there was a thumping in her ear, a palpitate throbbing that suppress the noise of whatever was closer to her.

Right at that very moment her blood pressure went up. And also , just the agonizing thought of the cartel catching her was horrifying, it was already starting to eat at her. They were called Drill Gang. She needed to smoke, to clear her mind, and process a few things. Needless to say she desperately needed to get to her safehouse. And that's where she'd feel safe.

# 10 Finger Discount

## Millennium Reedz

Breonna, now back at her condo after kissing up to her mother for about 45 minutes (with hopes of taking some pressure off her). She decided to walk down to the gym and get a nice exuberated workout in, (as Jenny tagged along). Seemingly the night was just now warming, (why not hang out with her bestie, she figured). In the mean time, Breonna switched her fit to something a little more appropriate, a black and pink Chisel Time sweat suit designed by GMG trainer. The fit looked impassively grand and it complimented her frame, with precise color contrasted. With the matching headband that sealed the deal-when you look good, you feel good, when you feel good you perform good, she confidently believed.

Along the way in the elevator, Jenny next reached in her purse and pulled out a novel, "yes girl you know how I get when I'm lit and in my zone," Jenn said.

As Breonna gave her the roll of the eyes. While opening up the novel that's about 210-220 pages thick. On the way down the stairs, the elevator was silent in the moment. Instinctively Breonna eyed the lavish cover since Jenny was standing next to her proximity. "Live From The Kitchen, huh? Since when you start reading action thrillers?" she said animatedly. "Ha-ha," she laughed while reading the book. "This is the best book I ever read," she added convincingly. Bing!

As the door opened, they walked briefly a few feet down a lighted hallway and made a left. There the gym was. Seemingly there were about 7 or 8 other people already using the equipment. Next stepping in to the a large exercise room, was a flat screen TV, 2 racks of dumbbells, about 4 weight benches, a boxing ring, along with several universal machines. However also toward the side exit there were 5 bicycles unoccupied.

As Jenny followed Breonna along the way, infatuated as her eyes still reading the vivid masterpiece in full delightment. Seconds later, Breonna didn't waste no more time as she jumped on the fitness bike and started peddling. Now on the flip side, Breonna planned on getting a gusto sweat, to keep her package nice, trimmed and tight. So she decided to do the bike for about 30 minutes, followed by a calisthenic workout that consists of 10 push ups, 10 jumping jacks, 10 mountain climbers, 10 tummy twists and lastly 10 squats, is all 1 set.

It takes willingness and dedication to keep her bonafide package ideal. Breonna more so had the workout routine engraved from when she played lacrosse, in high school. But in the fact of the matter, had she followed that path, she would have a promising career. Mid-way through her workout Jenny decided to go to take a ladies room break and buy a couple of bottled waters from the vending machine.

On the way to the restrooms, everything looked normal. Stopping just momentary to touch up her hair in a mirror on the way, it was inresseible. Stepping inside, a fruitful smell of strawberry air freshener gushed sweetly underneath her nose. Nonetheless once taking about a 10 minute tickle time break as she made her way to wash her hands and give herself a quick touch up with a light application of Mac make-up, out of complete coincidence, while she washed her hands standing in front of an oval shaped faucet made of ornate iron and glass.

From the parenthetical, she couldn't help but to notice the dark brown, tan, and cream colored Coach bag, placed on the floor next to another woman's stall. Devilish as the temptation crossed her mind, or was it the potent drugs playing with her mind. Then all a sudden Jenny snatched the expensive designer purse, and didn't look back. Dashingly eight steps afterwards she made a right, instead of the left that would've led her back into the fitness room. As she compelled the bag underneath her arm, with attempts of counseling if the weight of the bag felt like something of importance was inside she hoped. Abruptly just then, she heard a series of horrifying screaming coming from the ladies room. Over reacting with apprehensiveness, Jenny jetted out the gym and off to her car, peeling wheels doing a buck-80, leaving rubber particles all throughout the lot. SKRRRRRT!

# Living For Real in the 21st Century

## Millennium Reedz

Tay Tay at thirty two, he appeared to be more physically fit than he had been at 22. His home gym was well equipped, tip-top, in better words. Faithfully a personal trainer came to his house three times a week. On a Saturday morning in October, in his bedroom when he drew open the draperies and saw blue sky as polished as a plate. He went online to consult a surfcast site, and called Rolanda. In successions, she must have glanced at the caller ID readout, because she said, "good morning Haze." She occasionally called him Haze, because on the afternoon that she met him, 7 months previously, he had been extremely high off Kwiwe Jolly Rancher bud and straight Grey Goose. In keenly gestures Rolanda found it so sexy how he has a little edge about himself. His hazel brown eyes stared at her lustfully on their first encounter.

Sometimes when Tay Tay became so obsessed with making beats, that he went 48 hours without any sleep with attempts of creating the next-level sound, -is what Tay Tay reference it as developing a tenacious concentration unknown to most, he was very dexterous about his craft. Anyhow on a brisk cool fall day Rolanda had come to his studio to interview him for an article that she had been writing for Esquire magazine.

For a moment she had thought he was flirting with her and flirting clumsily. During that first meeting, Tay Tay wanted to ask for a date, but he perceived in her a seriousness of purpose that would cause her to reject him as long as she was writing about him. He called her only after he knew that she had delivered the article to the magazine company. "When Esquire appears what if I've savaged you?"

She had asked, "you haven't."

"How do you know?" Pausing for a brief moment, properly thinking her question before responding, "well for one I'm a great guy and for two I don't deserve to be savaged and I'm trusting you're a fair person."

"You don't know me well enough to be sure of that."

"From your interview style," he said, "I know you're bright, intelligent, meticulous, and free of political scandals. So in that regard, if I'm not safe in here with you, then I'm not safe anywhere in the United States of America." Have you ever lived in another country?" Rolanda said sarcastically but in a playful manner. He had not sought to flatter her, but there yet he always spoke his mind with straightforwardness. Having an ear for deception, Rolanda recognized his authenticity of the qualities that draw a bright woman to a man, truthfulness is equaled only by kindness, self-confidence and a sense of humor. Ultimately she had accepted his invitation to lunch and for the past 6 months, had been the ,most gailyly time of her life.

"Now on this Monday morning,"

he said scaling eight footers, straight and epic sunshine that ricocheted from the blue glisters of the blue sea. "I've got a deadline to meet."

"You're too young and beautiful for all this death talk."

"I've already seen your skill set and you're magically on the board. Yes I'm magically at times on my fresh days." "Totally phenomenal like with the shark." Rolanda complimented him as she sat apprehensively on the edge of her seat. "Oh- oh yes that was nothing," he said down playing the unprecedented ordeal as if it was normal news, "well that bastard bit a huge chunk out of my board." "I bugged out."

he said, "I'm under a funnel wave, in the dept's, grabbing for air, my hand closes around the skeg." (Which as the skeg, is the fin that melted on the bottom of the surfboard, in which holds the stern of the board in the waves and allows the rider to steer.)

Unknowingly Tay Tay actually grabbed the ferocious adult shark's dorsal fin. With eagerness Rolanda said, "who in God's green earth and on this planet dares to ride a bull shark?"

But all and all she knows the answer. "I wasn't just riding, I was terrified and undaunted all at once, it all lasted like only 30 seconds. I have unbelievable nightmares all the time reminiscing about this life and death situation." "Um-hmmm,

I am almost finished writing this article with, a sign of, he said are you ready, I'll meet you by the sur in a 45 minutes. Rolanda sighed in happy resignation. "45 minutes and wear the gold one," he said in typical fashion and then hung up. "The water should be warm, and the day warmer."

Tay Tay said but to no one in particular. It was obvious that he could leave the wet-suit. He pulled on a pair of throses with yellow ducks all over. Also in his collection included a pair with tiny shark patterns. If he would to wear them, she would talk a little shit, figuratively speaking. Being two-steps ahead of the game, for later in the afternoon he took a change of clothes in his GMG (Gorgeous Money Getters) designer sports bag, along with a pair of dark brown espadrilles.

However then next of the 3 vehicles in his garage, an on the year 2022 Jeep Wrangler cream on white, with t-top windows and heated gear shifter seemed to be best suited for today. Already stowed in the back, his board protruded past the lifted tailgate. Without even checking the 30 round F&N 45 Millennium he always kept was ingeniously stashed underneath the floormat. Before placing the key in the ignition, he centered himself comfortably. Just right before starting his Jeep Wrangler, he then pulled out his gas stash, to retrieve an already rolled hunny leaf of strong,( fruity-pebbles-sour that was top shelf cannibus ). With just the flick of a lighter, the flames attacked the leaf violently. In successions with a light pull the strong fumes entered his lungs. With instant gratification, Tay Tay blew the smoke out the t-top. At the end of the elegant brick-stoned driveway, as he turned left into the street, he paused to look back at the house.

Flawless architecture sloped roof of red barrel tile, gem-stoned walls, with glistering windows with panes of beveled glass reflecting the sun as if they were jewels. Diligently the landscapers trimmed the outgrown limbs that were espalred on the walls flanking the carved limestone surround at the main entrance.

It's true that anything in America is feasible, in just less than a little over 5 years, Tayon had gone from a tight, couch, roach infested one-bedroom apartment in Jacksonville's slums to the prestigious upscale homes high above the Pacific, life was good. Rolanda on the other hand , could take the day off as a given because, seemingly she was a writer who from totally persevering and industrious contributions could set her own hours. But on the contrary, Tay Tay could take off too, because he was opulent. Quick wits and hard work had brought him from nothing, straight to a winning situation. Momentary as he drove out of the gate-guarded community and descended the lakes toward Jacksonville valley, where hundreds of boats were docked and moored in the glimmering by sun gilded tides. Roundabout 10 minutes past by and he transitioned from Jacksonville Blv. to Looney to Sunshine peninsula which separated the harbor from the sea. Cruising toward the peninsula point, joyfully as he listened to the prolific Jay Z,. As Reasonable Doubt pumped modestly through the system, as you could hear a light thump from the Kenwood 12's that pushed the exquisite sound. Eventually he arrived and parked on a treelined street with charming homes and carried his board to Jacksonville Merria main beach. The sea poured rhythmic thunder onto the shores, by this time Rolanda should already be there, at the front entrance, which was between the harbor and the pier. Her above-garage apartment was a 4-5 minute walk from here. Seemingly she too had come with her board, a beach towel, some knick-knacks and a small cooler. It's early June and the summer is at full effort with temps in the mid 90's all week, touching the 100's. The firement is glowing with only a thin layer of clouds in sight.

The seagulls soared in the air, enjoying a cool relaxing breeze.

Meanwhile there she was, she wore a prodigious golden bikini designed by Versace. She was as perfect as a mirage effortlessly beautiful. She stood just over 5'6, long brownish tan hair that casada all the way down past her backside. Her black and Irish decent was bonifide to the sight. The two dimples on each side of her face clearly embellished her features. The sparkling golden patented around her neck had transparent diamonds, that dazzling in the light.

Rolanda had the body of a model from her flat stomach to stunning curves, that deserved nothing less than a dime. Her 34-32 B cup frame enhanced her springfullness personality as well. "What are they loafers?" she asked. "I see you styling playboy," without even responding. He reached in and gave her a passionate hug and kiss on her electricied lips. As their lips entwined, the wind blew soft strands of hair all on to his face. Soft and hot the sand shifted underfoot, but it was compacted and cool where the purling surf worked it screed. "I'm ready to go catch some waves!" she said. And with perspicacity he dashed off to the waters. In successions they launched their boards and prone upon them, paddled out toward the action. Raising his voice above the swash of the surf, he called to her, "I'm going out deep to grab a rip!" Her silvery laughter was heard next as she followed, loving a challenge. Within seconds and like on Q, consisted spaced waves came like boxcars, 6 or 7 at a time. Intervene between each set were periods of relative calm. While the sea was slacking, him and Rolanda paddled out to the line up. Next they straddled their boards and watched the first swell of a new set roll towards the break, with totally bewilderment she caught the second swell, on 2 knees, one knee, then skillfully jumping on both feet, swift and clean. In stellar fashion, she rode the crest, then did a floater off the curling lip. With intense momentum she slid out of view down the face of the wave, she thought that the breaker current was much, bigger than anything in previous sets had the size and the energy to hollow out and put her in an alloy. Good as it gets Rolanda would ride it out as smoothly as butter cooking in a pan. As the afternoon rolled on they had an outstanding time, exploring the Pacific ocean for it's adventurous world pool and tidal waves.

But there yet Tay Tay, saw the day dim, losing brightness at the periphery. But despite the horizon, the sky remained clear yet faded to grayish. Inky clouds spread through the jade sea, as though the Pacific would soon be black as midnight on Halloween.

# Safe Haven

## Millennium Reedz

While back on the Eastside of Orlando in Winterhaven section, the pair went to Jenny's apartment after the catastrophic ordeal that almost took both of their lives. "I can't believe we just witnessed that," Breonna said still quite shaken by the fact. Such pandemonium had her thoughts and nerves bouncing all over the place. Meanwhile, while over at Jenn's place, she freshened up and recollected her thoughts. At this point she changed clothes, that were suitable for the mode.

She was draped in a pair of Berry Berry volowers sweats with a powdered pink Royalty edition designer silk shirt made by GMG Apparel. Her lashes were natural and remarkably long just like a felion, with no shoes on, her feet with high arches was out effortlessly as she sat on the couch. "Girl are you alright?"

Jenny asked her friend briefly as they both were mesmerized, the room filled silent for a few moments. Institutively she fiddled around, flicking her wrist looking at her gold Rolex yacht master, it was a little past 4 PM. Moments later Jenn handed her bestie a glass of vodka with cranberry juice, to somehow help settle her nerves. Then suddenly, "Hurry up, hurry up, turn to the news!"

As soon as she turned to channel 10, the news report broadcast the reprehensively screen. 7 people dead, with another 4 in ICU. 3 SUVs and mini vans windows were blown out. Sadly even an innocent cat was caught in the explosion. Being conspicuous, Breonna could see her white Lexus in the footage and more so you could see the black Escattator speed wheels boisterous off the scene expendously. With them both pondering of whom it could've been. Just that instance Breonna remembered a short stocky chubby male standing a few yards from the restaurant.

Furthermore the blast left her right wrist swollen and it's throbbing some, "hey do you have any more of those double stack dolphins? Pleeeaseeee,"

She asked in the most adorable manner. Mimicking her bestie next Jenny dug in her purse, "bestie this is my last double stack, but I have some pressure,"

she replied displaying a fresh eight grader of spider white-widow bud, that actually looked like white fuzzy creepy spiders were crawling through the bag. Seconds later, she sprinkled some software, powdered cocaine, on top of the bud, making the perfect dink-blunt. Next taking a sip of her drink on the rocks, "Ummm these are my favorite 2 combinations," Jenny admitted energetically.

The reality of the matter was that they had just witness a totally horrific accident. But not with standing she added, "Ima call my boyfriend BBG and check on to see what he has for sale, I'm sure he can hook us up,"

she picked her phone and swiped lightly until she found BBG's contact. As the phone rung, she pranced around through her apartment juggling her bonifide ass awaiting a response. Jenny loved to freely ware comfortable boyshorts with no panties. Her double D breasts bounced limitless through the lush designer GMG apparel Betty-Boo edition spigget crop-top that she loves to wear. "Yo yo what it do," as a strong pitched voice answered the phone, "boy don't act like you don't see me calling your line," she spit trying to act presumptuous. "Naw, naw Jenny it's nothing like that boo," he said cooling down any tensions. "Umm, where you at?" Seconds later, "When can you come over?" seconds after that, "how long you gonna be?" Jenny asked all in rapidly fashion. "I'll see you when you get here then bae," she cheerfully said.

Meanwhile Breonna gazed out the 2 story apartment living room window. The view was panoramic, taking light tows on the strong dink-blunt. A dink-blunt is a mixture of weed and cocaine, which is classified as an upper. Some referred to it as a baby-WuTang. As the powdered cocaine sizzled and popped from the leaf like bacon in a pan. The fumes were egregious, as the skunk-ish smell filled the air. The scent lingered, smelling more like plastic being burnt.

With instant gratification, the dink blunt plus the ecstasy made her adrenaline rush in acute measures that flowed all the way down in her feet. Breonna was high as a barrel of oil, in a recession. Without any words said, Jenny approached and they began to play puff puff pass.

In total sic, they embraced the moment, enthralled in existence. You see in this way of life the drugs really takes it's efforts. Nevertheless hours later Jenny's phone rang. Neon lights bloomed form her I-Phone after a few rings, after taking a gulp of vodka, recollecting herself she answered the phone, abruptly without her speaking first, "I'm here," and the phone hung up.

# Blondie

*Bonus excerpt from LIVE FROM THE TRENCHES*

**Say hello to Blondie**

As Blondie awaits, it's a little past 9 PM, she's been sitting in her seagreen Audi A-4 outside Walgreen for the past ten mintues. With anxiety kicking in, she turns the new released ICE SPICE mix up a little more for safe measures. She'd been eariable all up until this point tonight, life wasn't to complexed nor complicated for the matter. You see , Blondie hasn't had any Addy 30's (adararl) in almost two days, which frustrated her tremendously. Usually, Blondies cohert and well organized, but the truth be told, the Addy 30's is what kept her compelled and level headed. That's why when her pill plugg called and said the strip would be filled later today, promptly she stopped every thing on her end and drove straight to meet up. Qualette was always reliable connect, she held a stift price and wouldn't bulge for nothing and Blondie respected that. In this world Blondie has a solid principles to adherence a code of values, that she would die honoring to respect. Which were; the gun; a true thorough-breed, and the hustle, in that order. Now on the other hand, Qualette was the definition of a one-stop-shop. Not only did she have the Addy's on demand, but could also hook you up with perk 10's, ROCKIES 20's, and the blue football Zanny bars, plus the E-pills were on deck as well. So whatever kinda day your trying to have , Qualette could make it possible for you. Only a 14-15 minute wait out in the parking lot, as a thick boned brown skin female, with full hips, fresh micro braids, and a exquisite ambush of tattoo's vigilintly covering her chest and neck, stepped out the drug store and started walking over and eventually hoping in the Audi. Apprehensively , Blondie hands had the judgers, as they swomp'd addys for cash. Instinciting popping the seal, tossing two addys in her mouth like some tactic's , as the car was quiet for a brief moment, "oh-gosh I almost forgot, I have some fire ass triple stack Pokemons."

Groping around in her Prada hand bag feeling for her pill stash. Opening her hands showing off her pills of joy. "Ok - why not."

Doing some quick calculations in her head, "then let me grab a ten pack."

Then next ,the two swapped drugs for cash. Blondie was relieved that her drug of choice was now back in her control. Seemingly as she watched Qualett walk past her car and entered her ford Milabo and desepearing into the night .With the pharmanceutical now kicking-in, Blondie felt electrify, she felt untouchable and most of all, she felt flawless. With instant gratification, the hairs on the back of her neck started to stick up as she peeled out the parking lot.

The V-8 engine, 5.2 liter, 10 speed and 469 horsepower, with heated steering wheel...burning rubber down military HWY, blowing past vehicles, SUV's and mac trucks, not worried about getting a speeding ticket.

Being a sweet innocent, god fearing half-irish / half-cacusina girl from the up scale part of OV (Ocean View), she has never been pulled over, or had never been in any trouble with the law, for that matter...Being oriniganly born in BOSTON,

MA, but her parents and she moved to Norfolk, VA. She was relutant of the fact, early on, but once she saw the 3-story level spanish mediterranean style home on the 16th Bay right on the beach , Blondie fell in love instantly.

Blondie is a gorgeous chick with exotic features that would always allures men and even females too. Her pellucid skin was flawless, at which you could tell she took delicate care of her personal hygiene...Her pink lips resembled rose paddles, with a button nose to match. Her lustrous hair displaying blond dread locks, that totally seperated her from the rest, her lustrous hair tickled her butt when she walked, as it swung from side to side. Her pretty green eyes, were adorable...the c-cup breasts' she was proud of, plus the ass she had, wasn't normal for a Irish girl. "God-damn that's a fat ass white girl," was what she heard every time she was in public. Momentary from the corner of her eye as a glow alerted her from her I-phone, that she had an incoming call.

Looking at the name - Spice Girl-, blinked on and off like a scary light. Effortlessly a slight grin slid across her face. Spice was one of Blondies closest friends. You see, 2 years ago when the FEDS did a sweep that indicted her lover, which ultimately ended up giving him 260 months, to serve, Spice witnessed first hand, as Blondie rebuild and orchestrated her empire. However their were plenty sleepless nights, many nights she would cry herself to sleep....

Quiet as kept , on one lonely night, she cried herself right into Spice's arms. Not trying to take advantage of the situation, Spice kissed Blondie on her plump red forehead, to her surprise, Blondie then opened her cat colored eyes and kissed Spice with wet and so-soft lips. What happened that night only remained amoust the two of them. Snapping out her frenzied, finally she answered "what's up sis?"

As she spoke into the mouth piece of the phone. "Damn a bitch ait gota hit a bitch back" referring to last night, when Blondie abruptly cutt their, conversation short, and told her that she'll hit back, half joking Blondie said, "oh shit my bad Spice, my mind was scattered around out of my wits last night, I really do apologize." Blondie respond in genuwin postures. "-umm humm," twisting her lips up in way that illustrating, a gesture saying she didn't believe her, one bit. "What's up tho?" Girl I'm out here ripping and road running", Blondie said.

Then taking a few mouth fulls of bottle water..."Maybe a mixed cocktail you know."

As Spice said getting straight to the point. "Are you trying to join me?"

Sounding like a delighted plan, Blondie agreed "where did you have in mind?" Well I had taste for a grilled shrimp salad from {The Palace}" she said.

Already knowing that exact spot, Blondie said "I'll be there in twenty minutes."

And the call went blink...About 20 odd minutes after, Blondie was walking up to the Palace, it's a bar and grill/lounge located in the center of Graby Street. This particular section is Shark City upper class.Its located downtown with all the innercity atomasphare , taking place all in one. McAuthor mall , (It's the biggest mall on the east coast), an division II college T C C (Tidewater Community College), there numberous other bars, strip joints, jewelery stores, and restuarants all packed tight on one long strip. Prestigious living at its finest.

As a luxuriant neighborhood Gent sits just beind this fleet of establishments. Judges

,lawyers, bankers, accountants, and important people of the elite, all mingle in this part of town.

Now in the front of the lounge Blondie handed the bouncer a 10$ to enter. The music could be heard from the front entrance. After a quick flick from the metal decetor she stepped in, lights were shinning in spectums and people were dancing. It was teatefully decorated with impeccable modern furniture, and it had a beautiful glass horseshoe bar. Already knowing Spice was in the building, so Blondie felt at ease, subsequently walking to the back bar, it was a mixed crowd in there, and it wasn't too jam packed. Then momentary, outa nowhere "heyyy - BFF?"

Spice said cheerfully, as she approached giving Blondie a tangible hug with a light kiss on the cheeks, which instantaneously made Blondie blush, they walked over to the table Spice already had occupied. "Blondie you look fabulous"

Spice complimented, (admiring her pink-ish red dreads), as Blondie returned the compliment confidently. Spice was laced in Chanel RED BOTTOMS, tight fitting denim capris, with a gold belt across her flat stomach. The blue/orange/ and pink GMG (Gorgeous Money Getter's apparel ), skulk bluse went brilliantly with her heels. "Excuse me, will the two of you need menus?"

As a brown skin waitress asked "yes" "please that'll be fine" Blondie respond flashing her lustering pear white teeth.

Momentary the waitress returned with the menu's, "what would you like to start off to drink" she asked. "Umm yes, I'll start with a matinee with lime please," and Spice entusiastic said, "I'll have a vodka and cranberry juice".

And the waitress dashed off...as the two cought-up on this and that. They singed along to the music, ate salads, and enjoyed the night. "OH dam, have you heard what happened to Shugg ?",."Naw - what happened to him?" Blondie asked giving Spice her full undivided attention" He passed away," Spice responded.

Blondie was utterly speechless initally while using both her hands to gesture her shock,"girl he died from having a stroke,".

Blondie started shaking her head in disbelieved. "oh and the cops have Boss Hogg locked up, for shooting a guy name China Man at the Jeezy show". Are you kidding me?"Blondie replyed.

She estatically remembers that night vividly, - she was too there-, saw the man stretched out on the floor, as a female held him helplessly .Meaningful Blondie she held the matinee starring at the lime through the glass, tiny tears dazzled in the corner of her eyes milked the silence even longer. "OH, I do have some good news."

Blondie raising an eyebrow inquisitvely, Spice continued on," well my phone plugg finally came through and dropped off ten brand-new out the box I-Phone Deluxe".

Jumping straight on it, Blondie put her bid in and pulled out her wallet to go ahead purchase, "ok now BFF, I'm saling them for 8 hundred a pop, but for you give me five."

As Blondie pealed off five blues and handed them to her with no hesitation.

Spice dilligently grabbed the cash and compelling it into her Ferragamo hand-bag.

"I got a couple of them in the car, girl I got you,"

as she winked at her closest friend. That was one thing Blondie admired, about Spice was that she kept a skeam cooking up. It's been numerous times that Blondie offered her fire batches of blow to sale, but reluctantly, Spice would always decline, she was more into the white color skeams and credit fraud -stuff like that- was what Spice get a rush out of.

Looking around at the crowd of people drinking, laughing, and just having a blast. "Girl, this is my song" grabbing Spice hands and they took the dance floor. The prolificent super star artist was playing as Plies rapped blasted through-out the speakers hit through-out the lounge, and the girls started boogieing. I got drip for sale aye / I got drip for sale aye.

Nevertheless after dancing to three songs maybe , next they headed back to the table. Checking her phone, Spice was happy to see, someone had hit her line, asking for an I-phone, while Blondie had a couple missed calls as well...Having a great time, Blondie didn't want to end the nice time, but respecting the paper, "sis I gota go bust a play," she spoke.

Furthermore Spice nodded in acceptance. Just before leaving Blondie was about to place a blueface on the table to cover their bill, Spice waved her off and whipped out a gold American express card, and took care of the tab.

After while exiting the lounge, cunningly a few dudes attempted to give cat-calls to the bonafide lady's , but being commented to the grind, they kept it moving. Receiving her brand new I-phone Deluxe, she walked a few paced to her vehicle, then out of the blue she heard, Blondie what's up?"

A dude spit out. Starred she slowed down to see who was calling her. In an friendly gesture the guy said, "it's me Dre,"

Where you been hiding at?"

She recognized the dude, he was from OV too, and he used to hustle with her dude a couple years ago. As he walked up in all black pants with a all black hoodie on, "where you heading off to pretty girl?"

Dam girl where you heading at so fast"?he said coyly . Im about to make a few runs , you know, besides I was just up in the Palace for a hot minute , alittle tipys but manage to say properly.

In peculiar postures stepping closer to Blondie , Dre insisted that they link up on another night . Looking around suddenly before looking down at her -plain jane- Micheal Kor's watch " I gota make some moves" . Making their fairwells subsequently jumping into the Audi A4. With the touch of a button , and the Audi roared like a Bagel Tiger / In audacious manners she sped out the parking space , Dre watched in amazement . Then suddenly , as Blondie jetted down Graby street , then in beguiling gestures his fake smile turned upside down , tight lipped , like a balled up fist , a smile that was now wicked...

The end...

Made in United States
Orlando, FL
12 October 2024